Assigned

Assigned

A NAVY SEALS OF LITTLE CREEK ROMANCE

PARIS WYNTERS

TULE
PUBLISHING

Assigned

Tule Publishing First Printing, July 2021

The Tule Publishing, Inc.

First Publication by Tule Publishing 2021

Cover design by Erin Dameron-Hill

ISBN: 978-1-954894-24-2

ACKNOWLEDGEMENTS

First and foremost, thank you to my Heavenly Father for blessing me beyond all measure. Thank you to my family for your support and encouragement. Thank you to my amazing agent, Tricia Skinner, for always believing in me. Thank you to Jane Porter and Meghan Farrell for believing in this series. Thank you to Sinclair Sawhney for pushing me to always bring the best of my characters out. I absolutely loved the way you helped guide these characters to be the best they could be. And thank you to Marlene Roberts-Vitale for all your support and insight.

A huge thank-you to Emily Hornburg. You continue to be a great friend and amazing sounding board. A huge, huge thank you to Eileen. You helped get me over those hurdles where I got stuck and couldn't figure out how to get across them, helped me figure out those stubborn words that were on the tip of my tongue, and helped me make sense of those things swirling in my mind desperate to get onto paper. And finally, thank you to my fellow Long Island Romance Writers group for always providing the motivation to keep pushing forward. You are all inspirations.

CHAPTER ONE

Lucas

DARK GRAY CLOUDS surround the last bits of blue in the sky like a predator circling its prey. A startling low rumble rings out as fat droplets rain down from the sky, cold and sharp on my head and shoulders. I turn up the collar of my jacket to keep it off my neck. The clouds close in, devouring the last of the blue, and with no break in the gray above, the chance of a letup is slim to zero. It's going to be a rainy day and no amount of pleading with God is going to change that. Best get used to it.

Besides, the weather fits perfectly with the way the week had been going. Mere minutes after arriving CONUS—back in the contiguous United States—life had smacked me upside the head like an angry mama with a misbehaving brat. Arriving home months after being deployed is never easy, but this, yeah, not what I had in mind.

"Lucas, are you even listening to me?" My ex-wife's voice cuts through my ruminations on the unfairness of weather fronts. I know the tone. I'm on her very last nerve.

I grind my molars and try to focus. "Lisa, what am I

supposed to do? You decided to move while I was gone, and now I'm expected to come up with a miraculous way to fix Mason's behavior issues?"

Mason.

My eight-year-old son. The tie between Lisa and me that would never bend or break, even if most of the other ones had. While I'd been gone, he'd moved to a new school, gotten in two fights, and been sent to the principal's office for talking back to the teacher. Lisa was at her wit's end and dumped it on me the second my feet hit American soil.

A loud groan cuts over the line. "I'm expecting you to get involved. To step in. No one said it was up to you alone to fix the problem. I've never done that to you."

My fingers tighten around the phone as my foot lands heavily into a puddle that has formed on the concrete walkway leading to the building my commanding officer is in. The cold water seeps into my boot. I swallow hard, knowing my next words will either start a fight or frustrate my ex-wife. Or both. "I have to go. I'll call you back once I'm done with my meeting."

She huffs. Frustration, it is. "Unless you're sent on a mission and then who knows when we'll talk again?" There's a long pause before she continues, and I sense the sigh on the other end more than I hear it. "But that's the way things go. I get it."

Without another word, she disconnects the call. My chest tightens. Nothing like failing those you care for. Again. Being a SEAL, I don't have the flexible schedules those in other careers may have. I can't push off a meeting with my superiors to discuss my son's behavioral issues in school. Those things have to wait, or Lisa has to handle them herself. And she has been. And she's getting kind of pissed about it.

I yank the door open to the three-story brick building that stretches across the center of the base and make my way to Captain Redding's office on the second floor. My stomach tenses as I trudge down a hallway lined with photos of former commanders. Today was supposed to be my day off, but for whatever reason, Redding needed to speak with me. ASAP. So here I am.

The secretary greets me with a nod as I walk in. The door to my commanding officer's office is open and he waves me in.

"Captain Redding. Sir."

"At ease." My C.O. places the papers in his hand down onto the big oak desk and leans back in his chair, looking me up and down with his dark eyes as if he's taking measurements. At fifty, Redding is still intimidating as fuck. Don't even think I've seen the man smile.

Ever.

He gestures to the two chairs in front of his desk. "Take a seat."

I ease into the one to my left, plant my feet solidly on the industrial-grade carpet, and wait for my commanding officer to continue. With the day I've been having so far, I don't need a verbal ass whooping to boot, but I'll take it if I have to. And since my best friend, Anthony Martinez, has been away at officer candidate school, George Redding has yet to find another person to dole out his frustration on. Though, let's be clear, Martinez was the cause of most of that frustration. I might just be guilty by association.

"Heard great things about your performance. You've earned a significant number of duty performance points. Between those, some vacancies, and your test scores, a promotion is in order." Redding tapped his pen on the papers in front of him.

Well, fuck. Maybe this day ain't so bad after all.

"Lucas, you work hard. You're a good man. Sure, when you and Martinez are together, Stephens may want to run for the hills, but there is a lot of potential in you, son." Redding drops his hand to rub his knee beneath the desk. We all pretty much have an injury or two that won't ever fully heal. It's part of the job. Redding is no exception. Rumor has it he blew the knee out in an op in Afghanistan, pulling a local out of a building that was about to collapse.

"Thank you, sir." I fight the urge to squirm in my chair. Redding is a man who would sooner swim naked through shark-infested waters than dole out compliments. So, something must be up.

"How's time home been treating you so far?"

And there goes the ray of sunshine. Poof. Like everything else on this rainy day. "Some things going on with my son since my ex-wife moved to Chesapeake with her fiancé. Trying to take care of it while I'm back home and have some time."

Redding nods. "Lisa's a strong woman. A shame things didn't work out between the two of you. But this job takes us away from our families a lot, so do what you can while you can."

I can't help but glance behind his desk at the framed photo of an older, attractive African-American woman with a younger man and woman in Sunday-go-to-church clothes on either side of her. Smiles light up their faces, and not the fake ones people put on for a picture. True, genuine smiles. Redding's walked the walk to keep his family happy.

"Yes, sir." I shift forward in my chair to stand when Redding raises his hand and signals me to stop. Crap, there's more.

He pulls a manila folder from the left side of his desk to sit in front of him and opens it. "Before you deployed, we had a conversation about you joining the Issued Partner Program."

Oh.

Shit.

I chew the inside of my cheek and take a second to collect my thoughts. While deployed, the military's spouse matchmaking program had been an occasional thought, something to keep me focused on the positives, instead of the atrocities I faced when outside the wire. Nothing like imagining who the committee might assign to me to become my wife.

It still baffles my mind on occasion that such a program even exists. But I can understand why the Issued Partner

Program was created. With the high divorce rates and some of the shenanigans that occur—like some idiots marrying their friends to move into better housing and out of the barracks—the higher ups needed to come up with a way to try and solve the problem. Still not sure why they decided on jumping directly to marriage instead of dating. Most likely operational security had a large part in that decision.

I looked forward to the virtual interviews, chatting with the therapists and social workers about everything from my goals for the next five years to how I liked to spend my R and R time. The program is something I truly believe in too. How could I not when two of my friends found love through it? I'd seen firsthand the way their partners complemented them in temperament and spirit. I'd seen the faraway smiles on their faces when they thought about their wives. Overheard the bits and pieces of conversations filled with warmth and laughter and desire and, yes, love. "Sir, yes. You recommended me and I signed up."

"Well, I also called you in today because a match has been found for you." Redding folded his hands across his middle and watched me.

Not the way I was expecting the day to go at all. Nope. What a freaking roller coaster. Instead of the elated feeling I expected at hearing the news I'd been assigned a match, my hands grow clammy and my heartbeat picks up speed. Redding was right when he said it was a shame my ex-wife and I didn't work out. She was great for the life. Supportive. Independent. Could handle things on her own. I never had to worry.

Only, our passion died out and even when we tried to fix it, the spark never came back. No amount of date nights, special lotions, or whipped cream in the bedroom could light that fire once it had gone away. We'd changed. Remained friends. Loved one another. But there was no chemistry anymore. No blushes. No inadvertent caresses. No breath that came fast and hot just from seeing her face. I'd come back from a mission and instead of falling into bed in a tangle of limbs and lips and hands and hair, I'd get a honey-do list and a hug. I might have been okay with that, but Lisa decided she needed—deserved—more. I couldn't exactly argue. I believed she did too.

For a while I'd been satisfied juggling my career as a SEAL and being a father to Mason. It more than filled my days and temporary girlfriends filled the nights I wanted filled. But when Martinez got married and wanted to go home to Inara more than he wanted to hit the bar, I found myself craving a partner once again. Someone to come home to who desired my presence as much as I did to be in theirs.

Shit.

Should've talked to Lisa before I deployed, informed her I'd signed up for the program. But things had been crazy with her engagement and my pre-deployment training. And a text was not the way to inform my ex-wife of my intentions. Just one more thing to add to the list of ways I let her down.

Not that I mentioned anything to my parents either.

They'd been upset over the divorce. Think my mom's been secretly hoping we'd get back together, which is also why I hadn't told them my ex-wife is engaged to someone. Though, maybe Mason mentioned it to them. But surely if they were aware they would have mentioned something to me.

My gaze falls to the folder on the desk. Blank and smooth, giving no hint at what might lie inside it. Would the woman assigned to me be a good fit? Would we have a great friendship like I had with Lisa and yet be able to keep that spark? Would there even be a spark in the first place? My muscles tense and the corner of my eye twitches. An image of freckles across an upturned nose and honey-blond hair dances through my brain. I push down the old memory from high school, from the girl who had taught me what love is and had then turned around and taught me all about heartbreak.

"Lucas?"

"Sorry, sir."

"You turned green for a second there. Are you reconsidering your involvement in the program?" He tilts his head to one side, appraising my reaction. His furrowed forehead and tight lips are noticeable even within the creases of his sun-weathered face, a sight that ratchets up the anxious energy bubbling in my chest.

I clear my throat and straighten in my chair. "No, sir. Just an old memory. So, the committee assigned someone to me?"

Redding shuffles through the pages and reads for a second. "Sure did."

This could be a win-win for me and my son. The program has been mostly successful across the board making matches for people, and having someone at home could benefit Mason. I wouldn't have to worry what to do if training ran late or if there was a last-minute exercise. Not that I would have this new person taking care of my son right away. I'd want to make sure I could trust Mason's well-being with her first. And Mason would need time to get used to the idea. At least now the possibility exists for him to live with me a couple of days during the week.

My eye twitches again. Not that I hate Lisa or anything, but the move certainly changed all of our lives. When we lived close to each other, Mason stayed with me on as much of a consistent schedule as could exist with my job because his mom lived a few blocks away. But now, it's a trek. Yet—as she has pointed out to me more than once—she has to move on with her life. Her world can't revolve around me, especially when I can't be present as consistently as I want to be and still do my job.

I fidget in my chair. "Um, sir. Can I see the file? Who is it?"

Redding picks up the folder and hands it to me across his desk. "Some woman named Riley Thompson."

The folder falls through my hands, the papers scattering onto the floor below. No. Fucking. Way.

No way it's that Riley. Maybe there's more than one Riley Thompson because it would just be the rotten cherry on this crap sundae of a day if it was the Riley Thompson of the freckles-and-golden hair variety, of the ecstasy of first love and the sucker punch of first rejection. It can't be her. What would she even be doing here? She should be back home in Texas.

But as I bend over and scramble to scoop up the papers, her picture comes into view. My vision tunnels and sweat beads on my forehead. While it may be fifty-five degrees outside, the office temperature must be at least five thousand Kelvin.

I close my eyes and take a deep breath as I sit up, placing the folder in my lap. "Sir, is there any possible way the committee could reassign me?"

Redding's lips press together, the lines in his forehead deepen, and his frosty eyes both narrow and become more intense. "The program isn't some app you can swipe left on. The committee goes to great lengths to correctly match individuals. What is the problem?"

What is the problem? How about the fact Riley is the girl who broke my heart in high school? Or the fact she's the reason I left town and joined the military. And let's not leave out she was the first, if not the last, woman to make me wonder what I even had to offer. "Riley isn't a stranger. I grew up with her and I don't think we're a good fit."

Redding groans and rubs his hands over his face. "You don't have a lot of options here, Lucas. You can get on board. You can reject the match, put yourself back on the wait list, and risk it taking years to find you another match—if the program is even around that long. Or you can pull out of the program. And I'm going to be honest here, son. The committee has determined you and this woman are a good fit. They might not take too kindly to you stating otherwise without even trying, and they might just kick you out of their own accord."

He didn't have to say it, but the inference was clear. Rejecting the match would also mark me as someone who didn't cooperate, who wasn't a team player. Not exactly great qualities in a SEAL. Especially after I volunteered for the assignment. All the work that had made Redding talk about promoting me just now could be for nothing. Out the window, as if it had never happened.

I slump as much as I can into the chair. I'd been right in thinking the weather had been an omen. The universe was well aware of what would be happening. Gray skies and pouring rain matched the way my life was at this very moment. Did the committee choose the weather too? Along with matching me with the one person I'd rather not see again in my life?

I sift through the papers, not really taking in any of the information inside, thinking back instead to the time we'd spent together. Sure, she broke my heart into tiny pieces and stamped on them with her saffron, Converse Chuck Taylor-covered feet. But she'd also been a caring person, especially compassionate to the animals on her family's ranch. I'd seen her bottle-feed a baby lamb with the tenderness of a mother with a newborn and calm a frightened horse with just the sound of her voice. She'd always had a kind word for everyone, a smile that lit up rooms. If that part of her still existed, I would be able to trust her with Mason, even if I couldn't trust her with my heart. That I would keep protected with a guarded perimeter she'd have to blast her way through.

And one thing is for sure. My son needs my help. There's been too many changes and he's not adjusting well. He's acting out. With the divorce, moving to two new houses, and going to a new school, I can understand why. So, if I get on board with being assigned to Riley, it could allow Mason to visit more often to hang out in the neighborhood, and bring more stability into my home, which could help with whatever issues he's having.

Hopefully.

I straighten up in the too-small chair. "Sir, I'm on board. I'll give it my best shot."

CHAPTER TWO

Riley

OF ALL THE crap luck. Lucas. Lucas-freakin'-Craiger is who this military committee figured I would best be suited for, the man I should marry and spend my life with. Not that they're wrong about us being good together. Or at least once upon a time, we'd made a great couple. Before my life took a turn toward the shitter.

Literally.

As Lucas carries the last of the boxes down the narrow hallway of the building where I'd been renting a studio apartment, I stare at the way the gray T-shirt hugs his broad shoulders and muscular back for far too long before averting my eyes. Talk about uncomfortable. Here I am ogling my ex who is now my fiancé, who's muttered all of two sentences to me.

"Luc, I'll meet you downstairs. I want to do one last sweep to make sure I have everything." And take an extra moment for myself. To cleanse my brain of any wayward thoughts and reevaluate my sanity. I should walk out now. I should run. I have my reasons for joining the program.

There are compromises I'm willing to make. But this is asking a whole hell of lot.

Lucas pauses midstride, twists his head the slightest bit to gaze at me with brown eyes I swear see right into my mind. I hope he didn't acquire any telepathic abilities since we dated, because the last thing I need is for him to read my reaction to his post-high school physique. He'd been cute at seventeen. Now he is something else entirely. Strong. Commanding. Chiseled. A man, not a boy.

My cheeks flame at the thought and I cringe. Great. Now I look guilty. But Lucas only nods before continuing on down the steps. Like I said, not talking to me. And here I thought it took couples several years of marriage to get to the no-speaking stage. We're overachieving already. Go team!

The thud of his boots on the stairs fades, leaving me time to mull over the question that's been plaguing me ever since he first appeared. If Lucas Craiger has no intention of communicating with me, then why on earth did he agree to be assigned to me in the first place? Or have me assigned to him? Or however this program works. Maybe I should have read a little bit more of the fine print.

I shake my body from my legs to my arms as if I'd walked into the biggest cobweb on the planet. But the motion does little to relieve the nagging anxiety, or the dull abdominal cramps making themselves known. I wince and put my hands on my stomach. "You know, I'd really appreciate if you could let me have at least a couple days of marriage before you start going off," I whisper to my midsection.

As usual, my GI tract doesn't reply. Maybe my gut and my groom should get together, seeing how they have that trait in common. Except, my autoimmune disease is one aspect of this whole arranged marriage I wasn't planning to divulge to my future husband, much less my high school sweetheart. Who, thanks to some twisted trick of the universe, happens to be one and the same. I didn't tell him about it back then and I'm going to keep it to myself as long as possible now.

After exhaling a long, slow breath, I get back to work. I make my way around the studio apartment, opening every cabinet and drawer, checking around every corner for any stray belongings that escaped the packing boxes. Once I'm satisfied there are no socks hiding in the corner of the closet or toiletries lurking beneath the sink, I head to the door, but turn back one last time to survey the empty space. "Goodbye, safe haven."

Not really a safe haven. More like my own little lonely cave I could hide away in. Still, it had been mine and no one else's.

After locking the door, I head down the stairs, drop the keys off in the super's mailbox, then walk out into the parking lot. Lucas sits in his truck, a gunmetal-gray Dodge Ram that gleams in the sunlight, the bed neatly packed with my boxes and bags. Everything at right angles and secured by bungee cords, tucked in safe and secure.

The sight stops me in my tracks as reality kicks in. Lucas.

Me. Cohabitating. Once we unpack my stuff at his place, getting out of this arranged marriage will be much harder. Do I really want to go through with this?

My mind flies to the alternatives—or the distinct lack of them—and I blow out a shaky breath. Yes. I do.

I've been over my options a hundred times, and marriage in the new military matching program is my best bet to achieve my goal of independence—as much as one could call it independence, since I don't exactly have a normal life. Getting paired to my high school sweetheart doesn't change that.

I glance at the downcast turn to Luc's mouth and grimace. Even if my soon-to-be husband acts like he'd rather be MIA than married to me.

After straightening my shoulders, I stride over to the passenger door and hop in. "All set."

Lucas turns the ignition on and the vehicle rumbles to life. "Buckle up."

My head spins toward him. "Huh?"

"Seat belt. Put it on."

I snort, remembering all the times we raced down dirt roads as teens, him flooring the gas and me shrieking out the window like I was on a roller coaster. "Since when are you a stickler for seat belt safety? You certainly didn't seem to care back in high school."

His jaw ticks. "Long time ago. Was a stupid kid back then. We were lucky we didn't get hurt. Now, please put on the seat belt so we can get going."

Careless, maybe, but never stupid. No. Not careless either. Maybe *carefree* is the word I'm looking for. This man looks like the weight of the world is on his ridiculously broad shoulders. Though, the paperwork the committee sent did say he was a father. Maybe this whole vehicular safety routine stems from parenthood.

Great. Just what I need. Another *parent* thinking they know what is best for me. Which is exactly why I didn't mention joining the program to my parents and have no intention of telling them anytime soon. Wonder if I could get away with them ever finding out for the rest of their lives.

I reach over and pull the seat belt across my body, then buckle it into place and give him an "all set" nod. Lucas waits until he hears the metallic click before pulling out onto the road. At least it isn't raining today like it has been all of last week. This move would've sucked even more than it does now if that were the case. I try to be grateful for the small blessing.

I open the window and let the cool breeze whistle into the cabin. Apart from normal street noise, that's the only sound as Lucas steers us down the road. Uncomfortable with the uneasy silence, I fidget with the seat belt strap until I can't take it anymore. "Lucky to have such mild weather. Can you imagine moving in one hundred-plus degrees?"

"Nope."

Just one word. Okay. Enough is enough. I turn to face Lucas dead-on. "Look. We're supposed to get married today. Sure, it's not in a church surrounded by family or even a little Elvis chapel in Vegas. And I get we have history, but you had every opportunity to reject us being put together. And you didn't."

He stares dead-eyed ahead, his chiseled profile void of any emotion. Nothing. Not a twitch. Not a blink. Must be the SEAL training because the Lucas I once knew was full of life and I could read every emotion on his face.

Or someone hurt him badly enough to make him shut down.

There's an unwelcome twinge in my heart at the thought about what responsibility I might bear in this situation. Maybe the someone who hurt him was me. It's been more than a decade since we were together, though. We were kids in high school. Plenty could have happened between then and now. For all I know, I'm barely a memory of his childhood.

Our future together, however, is very much my concern. "Lucas, you spent most of the morning loading my belongings into your truck without talking to me. You reached out via text message to discuss the living arrangements. Is this really how it's going to be?" I cross my arms in front of my chest.

He exhales loudly through his nose. Moments pass without him responding. I readjust myself to face forward and glare out the windshield. I've all but resigned myself to a silent car ride when the dumbass finally decides to express his thoughts. "How long you been out this way?"

Ah, darn.

Maybe I should've prepared for this conversation. I can imagine how it looks from his perspective. He should know I moved to Virginia from Texas before I signed up for the program, though. Being local to him was a matter of chance. I didn't know he was here. I mean, I knew he'd joined the Navy, but he could have easily been stationed in San Diego or any of a dozen other states. "Don't flatter yourself thinking I moved here because I knew you were stationed on this side of the country or anything."

"Wasn't. Asked a question."

Fine, then. "I've been here almost a year. I wanted a change."

He snorts. "Yeah, living in a studio apartment must've been some change."

I whip my head sideways and glare at him, my top lip twitching. "Why, because my parents own a big house? Their own ranch? They worked hard for that place and I worked alongside them. I'm not some spoiled brat. You know that."

For the first time, his mask of indifference falters, only not in the way I'd hoped. His lips press into a thin line and his nose scrunches, like he smells something sour. "Nice try, Cupcake. Did you selectively forget what you and your parents told me the day we broke up? How I would never be well-off enough to take care of you . . . with my family being from the local trailer park and all. You all said I'd never have anything good enough for you and I might as well face that and get the hell out of your way."

That's by far the most words he's strung together since I

set eyes on him today. Now I'm sort of wishing he'd stayed quiet. I fold my hands in my lap while my chest tightens and my heel taps the floor at high speeds. It wasn't exactly a day I was likely to forget. I'd been standing on the landing of the grand staircase that led from the foyer of my parents' house to the second floor. Lucas had been standing on the ground level looking up at me, like Romeo looking up at Juliet. Then my dad had said those hateful things and I hadn't bothered to contradict him. But that was more than ten years ago, and I'd had my reasons. I still do.

In fact, the real reason I broke up with Lucas directly relates to my reasons for agreeing to this arranged marriage. What a crazy, fucking circle this is. Lucas knows none of this. I couldn't tell him then and I can't tell him now. If only circumstances were different, but they're not.

"That was a long time ago. People grow and change. I'm certainly not the same girl." The words are truer than I care to explain, so I continue. "Can we move on? Or do you intend to use the program as a way to punish me for something I did when I was seventeen?"

A second passes. "No, ma'am. Not looking to rehash the past."

The conversation ends and we fall back into an uncomfortable silence. Lucas doesn't even flip on the radio.

I tilt my head away from Lucas, to hide my grimace. The abdominal cramps aren't so mild anymore and I pray a flare-up isn't on the horizon. It's a pipe dream, I know. A flare-up is always on the horizon. My Crohn's has never been completely under control, which is why I joined the program. Health insurance is expensive. My parents would have kept me covered, but that came with a difference kind of price—my independence.

They want me tucked away in their house under their watchful eyes, like a figurine on a shelf. As if I were some kind of fragile porcelain doll that might break if allowed out into the world. I get it. They love me and they took care of me through so many surgeries and treatments. It had taken a toll on them and on me. There were times I didn't know if I could go on, but I did. I got through it. They never seemed to be able to let go of it, though. They never stop treating me like I'm sick.

I know part of it is their guilt over my sister, Michelle, who died when she was twelve years old. She'd been out in the barn, mucking out a stall, when she was hit with a sudden onset asthma attack. My mother never forgave herself for not watching her more closely, not being able to get her help in time, and she swore she would keep better watch over me.

That had been fine when I was seven, right after Michelle died, but I'm a grown woman now, and I can't spend my life under my mother and father's watchful eyes. I want a chance to enjoy the times when I'm not sick, when pain and fatigue don't sideline me from everything else women my age get to enjoy.

So, I packed my bags and moved to Virginia Beach. In return, they dropped my insurance coverage since I no longer worked at the ranch. They probably believed that would have me running home. But nope. I was determined to make it on my own.

Turns out, independence is a heck of a lot easier to achieve when you don't have a serious autoimmune disease that requires routine medical care and expensive drugs. Finding a job while managing constant GI flare-ups has been a mess and the money in my savings account is running out. Now the current medications that had stabilized me over the past few years have stopped working. There are other drugs, other treatments, but not with cut-rate health insurance. No. A person needs the good stuff for those treatments, the kind that comes with being married to someone in the military.

I'd been about to pack it in and head home when I heard about the Issued Partner Program. So yeah, I joined. I needed to. For the medical benefits. And even if it doesn't last, the program gives me a chance to get a tiny slice of that big pie—a husband and a home—while also buying me some time to obtain the financial and health insurance security I need to become independent. I mean, a job must exist that not only will offer me my own damn insurance but also be flexible when it comes to my disease.

I figured I could do a year with someone. Lieutenant Graham said the level of intimacy would be completely up to me. Being someone's married roommate sounded a whole lot better than crawling back home with my tail tucked between my legs where my parents would suffocate me to death with their concern.

And I can't. I just can't. I've missed out on so much of life already because of my disease. Spent years in and out of hospitals. This is a gamble I have to take because I'm not sure living the other way is worth it.

And who knows? It could work. Maybe it wouldn't be for just a year. Maybe the military really had discovered a scientific way to find love. Only, I was matched with Lucas Craiger. I glance at his stony expression out of the corner of my eye. My chest burns with guilt. I hate the fact I'm essentially using him for the military medical benefits, but if I want a chance to experience all the things I've dreamed of since I was a kid, I need Lucas to get access to more expensive treatments, like the biologics Medicaid won't cover.

Until I can find a more permanent solution that doesn't rely on my parents.

As if...because that would mean pretty much handing them a reason to be overly intrusive. No way are they just going to hand over money without inserting themselves into my business.

For now, here I am. About to trade vows with an old boyfriend who thinks I'm shallower than a kiddie pool.

Should make for barrels of laughs.

"We're here." Lucas pulls into the driveway of a two-story house.

I take a deep breath as my eyes scan the property. From the glass storm door to the colorful landscaping, it's a far cry from the trailer park where he grew up. The house, with its beige siding and shutters on every window, is inviting.

Especially with all the flowers along the front of the house—pink peonies, dahlia bulbs in various colors, and even some marigolds.

Different from my parents' home too. Smaller. A lot smaller. I grew up on a horse ranch, with an expansive acreage and a huge, gurgling fountain near the circular driveway that led to the ornate front doors. I want none of it. I'd left all of that comfort behind for a reason. I don't want to live in the past. I want to find joy and meaning in the present.

I glance over at Lucas. There was a time he loved me, maybe too much. And I'd loved him. Might there be a chance he'd be willing to leave the past behind? To live in the moment with me? To make this work for a while? At least, until I could take care of myself? It doesn't have to be love. Can't we at least be friends?

Lucas cuts the engine and turns toward me. "Let's get some of your stuff inside before the officiant shows up."

I nod and hop out of the car. After grabbing my purse, I head toward the tailgate of the truck and pick up a smaller box, then follow Lucas up the walkway. He balances the box he's carrying on a knee as he unlocks the front door. I follow him in.

The house smells like being at the ocean, along with a sweet citrusy scent, as if there were a bunch of Starburst candies lying around. I take a deep breath in and some of my anxiety fades from the aroma alone.

"Like it, huh?"

I open my eyes to find Lucas smiling at me. The expression softens the harsh lines of his face, reminding me of teenage Lucas and causing my heart to skip a beat. Time has been good to him. If anything, he's even more attractive than when we were kids. "What is it?"

"Blue Odyssey. It's a plugin by Glade." He turns and heads up the stairs.

Not surprised. Lucas always did enjoy the different aromas in my parents' home. Mother was always switching things up. From fresh cut flowers to candles to pine cones and whatever else she could find. Lucas's mom didn't have a lot of extra cash around to spend on things that weren't necessities.

I swallow and shake my head to chase away the thoughts, but when I gaze ahead, my eyes land on Lucas's ass. Christ. Not where I wanted my mind to wander, but I couldn't seem to force myself to look away either. Through his well-fitting jeans, I could tell his ass was round and firm, more muscular than when I used to slide my hand into his back pocket in between classes. My fingers twitch at the memory, a leftover reflex from when I used to reach out and squeeze it.

I dig my nails into the cardboard box instead. What the heck? Impulsive butt grabbing is a bad idea. Very, very bad. I'm in this situation because I need insurance, not to rekindle a romance with my high school flame.

By the time we reach the landing, my impulses are back under control. We stop in the small loft, and Lucas points to a door down the hall. "Bathroom's on the left."

"Thanks." I nod. "Is that my room on the right?"

Lucas stills like he's listening for something, and his jaw tenses again. When he doesn't speak, I spin around, looking for the source of his tension. But we're the only two in the house, so I'm not sure what just happened.

"That's my son's room."

"Oh. Mason, right." A mix of happiness and grief had washed over me when I read he had a child in the multi-page document that was sent over, just like now. The day I'd ended things with Lucas, I'd done so deliberately, because I hadn't wanted my illness to hold him back. It hadn't seemed right to saddle him with a chronically ill girlfriend, especially one who had no clue what her own future had in store.

That hadn't prevented my heart from shattering into a million pieces, though.

Now, I know more about what I want…and don't want. Children fall in the latter category. Not my own biological children, at least. I was glad for Lucas. Making sure he could have that kind of happiness was a lot of why I'd broken up with him.

I pull my shoulders back and inhale a deep breath, ready to avoid the emotions threatening to bubble up inside. "So, where am I sleeping?"

"My room." Lucas makes his way down the hall to our right as I stand grounded in place. My pulse accelerates while my mouth goes dry. When he reaches the white door at the end, he peers back over his shoulder, a mischievous grin stretching over his face. "Kidding. This is your room."

I squeeze my eyes shut. Thank the Lord. On so many levels. This whole situation isn't supposed to be a lifelong partnership. Sharing a bedroom would complicate matters, and my life is complicated enough already. At least he's joking around, though. It's better than him not speaking at all. A lot better.

I smile and head over to him, the abdominal cramps loosening their hold a little. When I walk into the spacious room I'm once again rooted to the floor in shock. The center of the room is dominated by a canopy bed draped with sheer white fabric dotted with tiny embroidered flowers. There are enough pillows on the bed to suffocate someone, all in different shades of orange: tangerine, apricot, peach. Each bedside table sports a lamp in the shape of the Eiffel Tower. A fluffy light-blue throw rug stretches across the floor. A pod chair with auburn cushions hangs in the corner. All of it is familiar. Too familiar. The furniture and décor bears a marked resemblance to my bedroom back home in Texas. There's no way the similarities are random. None. "Holy time warp."

Oops. That was supposed to stay in my head.

Lucas places the box down on the desk in front of two large windows, then turns and crosses his arms, his legs spread as he straightens to his full height. He lifts his chin and looks down at me. "There a problem?"

"No. It, uh, seems awful familiar, though."

He kicks at the fluffy blue throw rug. "I was trying to

make you feel at home. Never met anyone so excited to get furniture for her fifteenth birthday before."

My parents had let me redo my bedroom that year. There'd been no budget. Everything and anything I wanted. My choice of color and paint and furniture. The room had looked like a drunk unicorn had thrown up rainbows on it. Just like this one did now. I'd outgrown it years ago.

But Lucas had remembered. Not just that I'd redone my room, but exactly what it had looked like. That's . . . unexpectedly sweet. Even if utterly misguided. "This is really kind of you." I scan the white wooden furniture with carved floral scrolls everywhere and sigh. He still thinks I'm that girl, like time hasn't passed, that I haven't grown and changed. "I don't need to feel like I'm back in Texas to feel like I'm at home. And this had to cost a fortune, Lucas. It's too much."

His jaw clenches and he turns away. I've hurt his feelings. Not my intention at all.

He walks over and plucks the box from my hand before placing it next to the one on the desk. I nibble my lip. Something is off about all of this. Because while his motives might seem thoughtful and kind, the emotion exuding from him is anything but. Stiff shoulders, thin lips. Eyes that glitter with an angry fire. "I can afford it."

Ah. Now I get it. My hands settle onto my hips. If Lucas thinks for one second he's getting away with bottling shit up before we can even sign the papers, he has another thing coming. "Why'd you really spend all this money?"

He pushes the boxes around as if trying to avoid answering. But I bet I already know his reasons. Stupid, stubborn man. I sigh as I study his rigid posture. I have to admit, I'm also to blame. "Lucas, things were said when we broke up that shouldn't have been."

He spins around so fast I take a step back. "You think I purchased this crap because your father had to rub in my face how poor my family was? And how I'd never be able to take care of his daughter?"

Yup, that's exactly what I think. Especially now, when he's glaring at me like I just punched a baby. But saying as much might make matters worse and being the officiant was on his way, fighting at this exact moment wouldn't be the greatest idea. "I don't want to sound ungrateful. I just mean, I know you said you wanted me to feel at home, but you didn't have to splurge on me. A bed and dresser from IKEA would've been fine."

At first glance, his face holds no expression, no emotion. But when I look closer, I notice his eyes are dark, smoldering even. His chest rises and falls with each breath, and after a minute, he finally speaks. "How 'bout we get the rest of the boxes?"

"Sure." Anything to escape the tension in this space. Even huffing and puffing while lugging around boxes sounds better.

We head out of the room. So much for thinking Lucas could leave the past behind us. I thought maybe we could be happy as roommates. Maybe even become friends once again. That we could make this time tolerable at least. But no, his bitterness over our breakup is going to trash any chances of that happening.

I sigh and make my way back down the stairs. If only things had been different, and I'd never gotten sick. Maybe Lucas and I would have stayed together all this time, maybe not. Either way, I doubted he'd have grown to despise me the way he clearly does now.

But life had other ideas. And now I have to figure out how to play with the cards I've been dealt. At least I don't plan on condemning us to this marriage for long. Eventually, we can both go our separate ways and truly put our past to rest for good.

CHAPTER THREE

Lucas

I'M ON EDGE and antsy as I stomp back to my truck, like all of my nerves are misfiring, and I could use a good workout to chill the fuck out. Riley in my house is causing my head to spin, among other things. She always did have that effect on me. Never in a million years would I have expected her to pop back into my life like nothing ever happened. To be my second wife no less. Talk about crap luck. And yeah, as much as I didn't want to admit it, what her father said that day did stick with me. It *was* why I'd purchased the real wood furniture instead of the cheaper prefab stuff. I wanted her to see from the get-go I could take care of her just fine.

But it's more than injured pride or a need to prove myself. I'd loved Riley, and her lack of faith in me back then had cut deep. The way she'd stood up there on the landing above me at their big old house and never said a word as her father had dressed me down and made it all too clear what he thought of me and my family and my prospects still cut me. My heart took a long time to mend. If it ever did.

Along the way, I'd entertained a few elaborate fantasies. Scenarios where I became a wildly successful entrepreneur or movie star, and Riley's family lost all of their money in a big scandal. In my dreams, she'd come crawling to me, begging me to take her back. I'd look down my nose and tell her, sorry, but she made her choice. Now she had to live with it.

All of my fantasies somehow ended with me flexing my biceps and leaving with the one girl she'd always hated, Bailey Landry, stuck to my side like Krazy Glue.

In my defense, I was still a kid at the time, and teenage boys aren't really known for having class.

But I'm older now. Married, divorced. I even have a kid. So while I've never forgotten how awful Riley and her dad made me feel in the past, that doesn't give me an excuse to be a full-on dick now. Fate has decided to bring us back together. Seems the least I can do is help her feel at home.

Even if her presence is damned distracting.

Besides, picking her up in that tiny apartment and bringing her to the four-bedroom house I bought with my own hard-earned money is at least a little taste of that fantasy. I cast her another sidelong glance while she's busy grappling with another box, frowning. I'm still not sure why she left Texas to begin with. And that studio apartment of hers . . . not where I'd expected to find her living. This picture is not adding up. She's not telling me something.

We trudge our boxes back up the stairs and into the guest room. I place the one I'm carrying on the bed before surveying the space with a critical eye. As I take in the white wooden dresser, bed, and desk, heat creeps up my neck. Fucking hell. Riley has a point. The bedroom is a close match to what I remember of her old house, right down to the layout. I'd even placed the bed on the opposite corner of her desk.

It was a girl's bedroom. Not a woman's. I'd meant well, yet managed to screw it up again. Story of my fucking life.

I rub the back of my neck. "Okay, I see it now. We can switch the room around if you'd like. Get different sheets and stuff."

She leans against the dresser, wrapping her arms around her abdomen, color draining from her face. "It's fine. I didn't mean to snap. Just everything took me by surprise."

She says fine, but her body language doesn't match the words. Is the room really that upsetting? I scratch the top of my head and think of something to say, something to ease the tension. "Why don't I give you a tour of the rest of the house, so you can find your way around when I'm at work?"

She nods and hoists herself upright. When we step out of her room I point down the short hallway to our left. "My room is there."

Then we pad down the hallway back to the stairs until we hit the main floor. Since the entrance of the house opens up to the living room on the right and the dining room on the left, I don't bother giving a tour, instead leading her into the kitchen. "Pretty standard kitchen. The island just has cabinets." She doesn't comment, so I fill the silence. "Stove is here on the right against the wall and the sink and dishwasher are on the left by the window."

I grimace and shut my mouth. I sound like an idiot pointing out appliances she can see for herself. Must be nerves. Despite our rocky start, I want Riley to like my house.

Still. I'm probably better off sticking to single word responses, like earlier.

Luckily, Riley doesn't notice. She's too busy admiring my favorite kitchen feature. "I love the table in the alcove. The bay windows makes it so appealing."

I chuckle, recalling the struggles of trying to get Mason to eat when he was younger. "Except for when you have a toddler who's too distracted watching the birds and squirrels in the trees outside to finish his food." I turn to leave the same way we came in. "Come on, let's head to the den."

We walk down the short flight of stairs to the lower level. I point out the other guest bedroom, the bathroom, and the laundry room. The entire time, I find myself sneaking peeks at her face to gauge her reactions. She's so damn beautiful. More angular than she was in high school, and not nearly as tanned, but with the same wavy blond hair, cerulean-blue eyes, and toned calves, which are bare beneath the loose, flowered dress she wears.

With effort, I tear my attention away from her legs as we enter the open area that became the den. "This is where we spend time watching TV or hanging out. Lisa wanted to have a place to entertain, which is why the living room upstairs has no TV."

Riley quirks a brow. "You mean she wanted one place for those who want to watch sports to disappear to without distracting those who would rather sit and talk."

A smile pulls at the corner of my mouth. "Something like that."

Riley walks around the room and stops in front of shelves surrounding the flat-screen TV to snag a framed photo. "Is this your ex-wife?"

Shit.

I walk over and look at the picture. It's one of Lisa, Mason, and me at the zoo from three years ago. We were happy then. Everything was great. We'd even been talking about having another child. How fast things change. "Yes, that's Mason's mom."

She returns the photo to the shelf. "She's pretty."

I nod. Lisa's a looker. Long, dark hair, tall and thin. But that's not why the picture's there. "She's my son's mom. I want him to feel at home here."

Riley steps back and toys with a loose strand of hair. Her gaze strays over to the photo again before darting away. "Can I ask what happened between you two? Why you got divorced? Was it . . . amicable?"

I take a slow, deep breath to stem the rush of defensiveness. I couldn't expect Riley to understand. She'd never been married before, or had kids. "Lisa and I didn't separate in some nasty way. She's a good woman; things just didn't go as planned."

I'm not sure what else to say about it. Lisa left because

she claims the passion between us fizzled out, but who knows? Maybe there was some larger issue she didn't want to share. After all, Riley ditched me without so much as a goodbye the first time, so clearly I was doing something wrong.

Riley gazes up at me with those clear blue eyes. Doesn't say a word, but even after all these years apart, I can still read her curiosity in the cute way she tilts her head. At first I bristle, then realize, why not? Maybe an explanation would help prevent a third relationship fail. "My job interfered with a lot. It takes me away from home too often, like across-the-ocean-distance away. Even when I'm here, my schedule is unpredictable. All that time apart makes it hard to maintain a relationship. I missed the birth of my son, holidays, lots of other important events. Eventually it drove a wedge between us, and we went from being lovers to friends. The passion was gone."

Even though I'd felt the distance between us, too, I'd been willing to fight to get us back on track. Lisa hadn't. She'd been done. Ready to move on and find someone else.

My lips twist at the memory. The failure of my marriage still hurts.

Riley steps closer and curls her fingers around my upper arm. Her touch is soft, warm. Electric. My skin tingles in response. "I'm sorry. I bet that was hard on you and your son."

I edge away from her grasp, annoyed by my body's betrayal. I don't have to be a dick, but also, only a glutton for punishment would invite the first woman to ever break his heart back in for a second chance without showing some caution. "Sure can say that again. That's why I joined the program, and why I agreed to the match even when I saw your name on the paper. I don't want to bring a parade of women through my kid's life. I need a partner who can deal with this life and be there for me and for Mason." When my eyes start to burn, I tilt my head and stare up at the ceiling, hoping to chase away the tears that are forming. "The kid's had a tough time with the move and hasn't been adjusting well. It's not what I want for him."

Once I regain my composure, I look back down at Riley, to find her smiling at me. "You're probably a great dad. Your family was amazing, so caring, did a lot for one another. I remember those mandated family dinners every Sunday."

"Wasn't all sunshine and rainbows. They worked hard and still struggled to make ends meet. You know that." I shake my head. "It's why I started working at fourteen, to help out with bills and putting food on the table."

"Luc, I know. And your loyalty and selflessness to your family is one of the things I admired most about you."

Not enough to keep you from ditching me to find someone closer to your income bracket.

Although based on that crappy apartment she was living in, that didn't exactly work out so great for her. A bitter taste floods my mouth. I swallow and shove the memory aside.

As for my parents, maybe I should keep my current relationship status quiet. Who knows how this will turn out and my father sure as hell will read me the riot act. Whenever my parents visit, he constantly makes offhanded comments about how some of the more expensive things in my house were purchased for no other reason than because of the Thompsons. At least he's smart enough never to have mumbled his feelings in front of Lisa. But if he found out I was back with Riley…yeah, not ready for that.

And my past with Riley no longer matters, not when I have Mason to consider. Which means it's time to draw the line in the proverbial sand before the officiant arrives. "Listen, I'm not sure why you're really here. With me, no less. But as I already said, I'm doing this as much for Mason as I am for myself. If you are having cold feet or are here for a quick trip down memory lane, leave now. It's one thing to bail on me, but I won't allow you to do it to my son. Not that there is a guarantee this match will work. But if you are going to jump ship in a month, tell me now."

Riley pales and fidgets. Fuck. I groan and take a step back. Of course she hadn't intended to stay. While this house is far from the trailer I grew up in, it still doesn't compare to the fancy ranch she called home, although it's far better than that crappy studio she was living in. Which still makes no damn sense to me.

"Luc, I am not leaving in a month. And I assure you I will not do anything to harm your son. And I am certainly not here for revenge. I left you, remember."

She averts her eyes when she says it. Like there's something she doesn't want me to see. Before I can pry further, the doorbell rings. Lousy timing. Fists clenched, I stare at her for another moment, waiting for her to confess. To what, I'm not sure. But she remains silent, so when the chimes sound throughout the house again, I pivot and head upstairs, with Riley right behind me.

When I reach the front door, the officiant is waiting on the porch. The storm door creaks when I swing it open, allowing him to enter. "Thanks for meeting us."

A short, dour-faced man with a receding hairline and bulldog jowls squints up at me. "Where would you like me to set up?"

So much for pleasantries. "The living room should be fine."

Riley and the officiant head into the living room and I follow behind. We sit on the couch opposite the man, watching as he places his briefcase on the coffee table, then pulls papers from the manila envelope in his hand. He pauses while thumbing through them and glowers up at me. "No witnesses?"

"No, sir." While Jim and Tony both had witnesses, there's no statutory requirement that witnesses be present at a marriage ceremony in Virginia. And since I had no idea how things would actually go with Riley, I'd opted to keep our impending nuptials quiet for now.

The officiant mutters something I'm guessing is uncomplimentary under his breath.

Geez. Hadn't been expecting confetti bombs and back-slaps from the guy, but did he have to be such a grouch?

I steal a peek at Riley to see how she's taking all of this, but she's staring into her lap, her blond hair spilling forward and hiding her face. My muscles tense when I notice her shoulders shake. Oh hell, is she crying? Over our troll of an officiant?

Or . . . what if she's upset over the reality of marrying me?

My blood turns cold and my stomach flips, making me queasy. Before I can completely freak out, Riley sweeps her hair behind her ear. That's when I get a better look at her face, and comprehension dawns. Riley's not crying. She's laughing.

I let out a breath I didn't even realized I'd been holding. I'd forgotten how Riley had a bad habit of bursting into laughter at the most inappropriate moments.

I peek at our officiant, who clears his throat with a very dramatic *herm-herm* while drumming his fingertips on his thigh. I press my lips together tightly to fend off my own smirk. Once the need to chuckle passes, I return my attention to the man sitting in front of me. "I'm sorry, is there something I need to be doing?"

He heaves an exaggerated sigh, one that shakes his jowls in a hilariously awful way. A tiny sound escapes Riley, making my stomach clench. I squeeze my own hands in my lap and pray I don't lose it.

"The *rings*," he says, like he's irritated I didn't read his mind. "Have you received the rings?"

His question throws cold water on my amusement. Crap.

I'd been so brain fogged when I read Riley's name I forgot my envelope had our wedding rings in them.

Wedding rings. Holy shit. We're actually doing this. "Yes, sir. They are upstairs in my room."

I risk a glance at Riley. Her shoulders have stopped shaking, but now she's jiggling her leg, completely silent and looking everywhere but at me or the officiant. I place a hand on her forearm. "You okay?"

When she offers me a weak smile, she looks a little pale. "Just nervous."

The officiant looks between the two of us, then explains he is here to both witness our consent and to validate the marriage for legal purposes. I lace my hands together, palms sweating. The fact I'm about to get married again hits me like a wrecking ball. And this time I'm not so sure it's to the right person. I take a deep breath and remind myself this is for Mason.

Riley is in no better shape than I am, considering how much her leg is bouncing as we recite the vows, and how her voice rises in pitch every so often. When we finish, the officiant hands us a paper. "I need both of you to look over the marriage certificate. Make sure your information is accurate and then sign it."

I take the paper and glance over it. Everything is perfect so I grab a pen from the table and swallow past the lump in my throat as I scribble my signature on the empty line. Then I hand the certificate over to Riley. She chews her bottom lip as she reads over it, her leg bouncing faster now. She looks over at me, then takes the pen and signs her name. When she's done, she hands it back to the officiant, who completes his section.

As the man packs up his briefcase, Riley half-raises her hand as if she's in school and wants to ask a question. "Um, do you know when the medical benefits will kick in?"

I frown. What prompted that question? And why not ask me? I turn to face her. "Should take a couple of days. No longer than a week. Your name will also be added to my bank account and I'll have an ATM card for you too."

At that last part, her eyes narrow. "I don't need your money. I can take care of myself."

The officiant straightens and clears his throat. "Ma'am, service members have a financial obligation to their spouses. It's in the contract."

Riley blinks rapidly. "I, uh, it was confusing."

She was never one for details. Even in school, Riley was the person who would miss that a question had a second part to it and end up only getting half credit on her work. But I'd read through the contract. It's there for our protection. Nothing shady about it. Even if it took me a couple of read-throughs to understand the financial section myself.

She turns back to me. "I get it, but understand I won't be using the ATM card at all."

I shrug. "Fine by me."

When the officiant is done collecting his belongings, I walk him out. Once the door is shut, my gaze falls back to Riley, who is sitting stiff as a board on the couch, with no trace of the earlier laughter to hide her obvious misery.

My gut clenches as dread washes over me. Maybe this wasn't the best idea. Maybe I should've rejected the match and taken my chances . . . for both our sakes.

CHAPTER FOUR

Riley

I LIE ON the couch in the den, wrapped in an afghan my grandmother crocheted for me. It's a touch of home I'd brought to Virginia Beach. Thankfully, Lucas is at work. Definitely don't want him seeing me when I feel like shit. Nor do I need him asking questions either. Right now I can blame my symptoms on stress and he'd believe me. It wouldn't even be an outright lie, since stress often triggers episodes of autoimmune diseases. It started getting bad the day I moved in last week, with cramps coming and going during our "marriage ceremony," such as it was, and if that wasn't stressful, I don't know what is. Luckily this isn't a full-on attack. Just Crohns' way of keeping me on my toes and off my feet. Still, even this mild flare-up has been knocking me on my ass the past couple of days.

I pull the blanket tighter around my body and squeeze my legs to my chest as a wave of nausea washes over me. Seriously, FML right now. None of this ever gets easier. Once I believed it was possible. That my symptoms would weaken with time, or that somehow I'd learn to live with them. But nope. I groan and lean my head back. At least I've had the house to myself.

Speaking of, I've barely seen Lucas at all this week. Once for breakfast three days ago and twice in passing when I got up to use the bathroom late at night. If that's his work schedule while he's home, I can't imagine what life is like when he's away. My chest tightens. "No wonder his son has been having a hard time."

Growing up, Lucas and I both had our fathers around, even if they worked a lot. I really can't imagine how Mason is handling all this—the divorce or his dad's long hours away. How do any of these military kids handle a parent—sometimes both—being gone so much? Which is why as long as I'm here, married to Lucas, I plan to help Mason as much as I can. It's the least I can do. I doubt it'll make me feel like any less of a heel when I leave. Though just because I'd no longer live in the same house or be married to Lucas, doesn't mean he or Mason couldn't ask for help when needed. I still intend to remain in Virginia Beach after all.

It's just the marriage situation that's temporary, not my willingness to help a young boy or remain friends with my now husband.

My phone chimes go off and I grab it to check the time. I hoist myself up and slip on my sneakers. Time to go. Maybe this new doctor will be able to help me more than the last one I saw did.

I collect my stuff from the coffee table and head out the door into the garage. After starting my car, I turn on the

GPS and make my way out onto the road.

The drive isn't long and I open the windows, hoping the fresh air will help manage my nausea. Nothing like the tinge of salt in the ocean breeze to make me feel a tiny bit better. The bright sun warming my arm that rests against the driver side door is nice too. Maybe later I'll take a walk, if my GI tract cooperates. But only if no one else is around. No need to have strangers staring at me. I already know how pale and sickly I look, and I feel like utter garbage already without having to stress over introductions to Lucas's neighbors.

Fifteen minutes later I pull into the parking lot, turn off the engine and, after taking a few deep breaths to curb my queasiness, walk into the building. The office is bright, with eggshell paint on the walls and light wooden furniture. The seat cushions are a lime green along with the reception desk. I make my way to the self-check-in station and plug my information in before taking a seat.

"Mrs. Craiger."

I pull out my phone and start to scroll through the news when the receptionist calls out into the waiting area again. "Mrs. Craiger."

That's when it registers. Mrs. *Craiger*, as in, Lucas Craiger. Holy hell. That's me. "Um, yes."

I stand and make my way to the desk, heat rising to my cheeks. Totally forgot about my new last name. It sounds so strange.

"Ma'am, please fill out these forms. Also, we got your medical records from your previous doctor. Thank you for taking care of that ahead of time."

"You're welcome." Better to have the doctor equipped with as much information as possible rather than go through testing all over. Plus, hopefully, it will save on time explaining my past to him. I take a seat and fill out the paperwork, appreciating the fact I made note of my new address before leaving. How embarrassing would that be? Not knowing my own name or my address. When I'm done, I return to the receptionist and hand her both the paperwork and my insurance card.

"Take a seat and the nurse will call you when the doctor is ready."

I nod and do as I'm told. It's odd. Medical offices bring me a sense of calm, as if I'm in a safe place. Or a place where answers can be found. I don't feel the need to hide the fact I'm not doing so well while I'm here. There's no one judging me and no sympathetic or confused looks from people who don't get it. In a medical office named Digestive Disease Care Specialists, everyone can relate on some level to what I go through every day. Even the family members accompanying the other patients usually understand too. There's no need to put on the fake smile, no fake demeanor, no explaining. I can just be me. Riley.

The door to the left of the front desk swings open, and a couple emerges. The man waves to the receptionist before wrapping his arm around the woman's waist. I swallow hard. How would it feel to have a partner to walk by your side through the highs and lows of this disease? For a brief moment, I picture Lucas sitting in the chair beside me. But no. The reasons I sent him away all those years ago still hold true today. He doesn't need to be saddled with some sick girl. He has bigger responsibilities and broader horizons ahead of him.

"Mrs. Craiger."

A man in green scrubs waiting by the door rescues me before my imagination runs too wild. I raise my hand to acknowledge him, collect my purse, and walk over. We make a quick stop so he can record my weight—down another two pounds—and then head into an exam room where he takes the rest of my vitals.

"Doctor will be in shortly." He turns and walks out the door.

I glance around the room, reading the medical posters—posters I've read so many times I've lost count. Some of them list various medications available while others lay out the intestinal tract, pointing out what healthy looks like compared to various illnesses and diseases. Across from the exam table is a laptop. Hopefully, this doctor is one to pay attention to me first and worry about entering his medical notes second. Nothing I hate more than talking to the back of someone's head while they are typing away.

A moment later there is a knock at the door before it opens. "Good Morning, Mrs. Craiger. I'm Dr. Patel."

She extends her hand out and I shake it. Then she takes a seat at the computer. And I guess I'll be speaking to the back of her head. What I didn't want. But she looks over her shoulder. "No worries. I just want to go through some of your information before we begin."

Oh. Well, okay then. She runs through my height, weight, current meds and date of my last period. Once she is done, she spins the stool around to face me. "So, I went through all the records you had sent over. Quite extensive. And the surgeries. You are very lucky to be alive after the sepsis issue."

"Tell me about it. It's hard to forget. Of course, nothing like having a bunch of scars across my abdomen to remind me every day and to make me feel sexy." I clamp my mouth shut and my eyes widen, unsure of why I had just said that.

"Have you considered plastic surgery if the scars bother you so much?"

I snort. "What happens if I need another surgery? I would've wasted money then." It's not like I hadn't considered it. After weighing the pros and cons, I had decided the cons outweighed the pros. At least, they had on paper. The look of horror on a man's face the first time I take off my shirt doesn't translate well to a list.

"How are you doing now?" Patel asks.

I lift a hand and rotate it side to side. "So-so. Maybe having a mild flare-up. The past two days, I don't want to eat and keep running to the bathroom for one reason or another."

"Any changes in your diet? Life? Work?"

"You can say that. I just moved. And got married."

She smiles. "Well, congratulations. Stress can aggravate

cases, especially those like yours. Have you had any fevers? Or have you been febrile at all?"

I scrunch my face as I recall the few times I did bother to take my temperature. "No. Temperature's been normal."

"That is good. No need to put you on an antibiotic then. I don't want to use them unless absolutely necessary. But keep an eye on your temperature."

Dr. Patel stands and we continue our conversation as she conducts her exam. When we're done, she sits back down at the computer and begins entering in her notes. "Why don't we see if we can get you into the trial for this new medication?" She hands me a fact sheet with the name. I've heard of it. "You fit all the criteria including that you haven't improved on two prior medications."

"I'm down." Anything to help me get this disease under control, so I can start my slow climb toward independence. Although, given my responsibilities of helping to care for Mason, it'd be great to get this disease under control as soon as possible.

"All right, and if your symptoms don't get better in a couple of days, I want you to get a CT scan. The front staff will give you the orders. If you think you are going to go, just call the office for them to get the insurance approval first."

We finish up and the doctor exits the office. She gives me a refill for some anti-nausea medication and puts refills into the mail-order pharmacy the insurance makes us use. I sit up and take off the hospital gown, my hands skating over my heavily scarred abdomen. I huff, my muscles tensing. The moment Lucas sees the raised, puckered skin, he's going to ask questions. Lots of questions. And he's a smart man, so it won't take him long to connect the dots. I'll do my best to give him the least information possible.

I'm not the right long-term wife for him. I know how he takes on responsibility. There aren't many fourteen-year-olds that find work so they can help their mother put food on the table and keep a roof over their heads. I admire him for it, but I don't want to be one of those responsibilities. I don't want him to see me as the sick girl he needs to take care of, nor do I want him worrying when he should be concentrating on work. Lord only knows the danger he's in when on a mission. And I know if he finds out about my Crohn's, he'll worry, the same way he did when I got thrown from a horse at fifteen or when I broke my arm at a soccer game. I swear he was at my house every waking second he wasn't working or at school, looking for ways he could help.

I shake my head recalling the detailed notes he'd taken in class, including recording the lectures in case he missed writing something down. I don't want to be a burden to him. In fact, I need the opposite: to contribute for a change. But it's more than his worrying. Even if by some complete fluke, we end up as a couple before this "marriage" is over, I'd never put him in a position where Mason would have to be his only child. The risks to my health are too great to even consider carrying a child to term.

Wait, what? I've barely laid eyes on the man since we

signed our vows, and my brain jumps straight to kids? I can't think about this right now. Or ever. I grab my shirt and slip it over my head. The moment I stand, my stomach cramps, so I curl over and grimace until the pain passes. If I am accepted to start this new medication, maybe my life will finally begin to change. Wouldn't it be something to get these symptoms under control? A glimmer of hope sneaks its way into the gloom of the moment.

While I might not physically be feeling the best, there's a new spring to my step as I leave the office and head toward my car. After pulling onto the road, I flip the radio on and roll down the windows.

Everything seems to be changing, for the better. And for once I'm not preoccupied by my disease or drowning in pessimism. Outside the windshield, the world is brighter. The sun warmer. The ocean bluer.

The ocean. It's always been a place where I felt free.

My fingers tap to the beat of the music on the radio. With no real need to race home, I head toward Sandbridge. Too bad my surfboard, with its beautiful yellow hibiscus designs on a tangerine background, is back in Lucas's garage. Doesn't matter though, because sitting on the sand and soaking up the warmth will do fine. Just being by the water is enough.

After parking, I hop out and make my way toward the water. Well, maybe not having my board does matter because those waves look amazing. Kicking off my tangerine Chucks, my toes dig into the soft grains.

To my right is a canopy tent surrounded by young children. Most likely surfing lessons. I shift direction, curiosity getting the best of me. The big yellow banner attached to the front of the folding table confirms I was right. It's a surf school for "Gold Star" families, whatever they are.

"Where have I heard that term before?" A quick search on my phone brings up results and my heart lurches. A Gold Star family is one that has lost a member in service to our nation. They're the loved ones left behind when a service member makes the ultimate sacrifice and gives their life.

These are the children of service members who have died.

"Can I help you?"

My head jerks up from my phone to find an older man, his gray hair long enough that it covers his ears, waving at me from behind the table. After tucking my phone back into my jean shorts, I wave back. "No, sorry. I was just taking a walk and your banner caught my eye."

"Were you interested in signing your child up?"

My eyes widen and it takes my brain a couple of seconds to make sense of his question. "Uh, no. I don't have children."

"Oh. Do you surf?"

"Love it. But nowhere near being a pro or anything." Love it is an understatement, but I don't have a better word for how I feel about surfing.

The man laughs. "We could always use volunteers if you are interested. My name is Brian, by the way."

He extends the offer like it's no big deal, but to me, it's everything. Volunteering would give me a sense of contributing, of giving back. Make me feel like I am needed instead of being a burden. "Riley. And yes, I'd love to volunteer."

Brian hands me a clipboard with a packet to fill out. As I scribble in the information, the excitement pulses harder through my veins. This day keeps getting better and better. First a chance to join a new trial, and now a way to give back while doing something I love. It's another step to becoming the independent person I want to be.

Once I finish filling out the forms, I return the clipboard and thank Brian for the opportunity. I turn to leave and spy a small group of children standing in front of an instructor, who asks them what they know about surfing. The children call out different aspects and information they know. One of them mentions how his father surfed and follows up by telling the group how his father died.

My throat tightens and my heart aches for the child.

Then my mind wanders. *Mason.* Oh my God. That boy could easily be Lucas's son.

And Lucas could one day become that boy's father.

Tears prick my eyes. The breeze against my skin feels colder. I wrap my arms around myself.

Lucas could die because of his job. A fact I never thought of before. One I'm not prepared to deal with. A cloud passes over the sun and I shiver in the sudden shade.

So much for my postcard-perfect day.

CHAPTER FIVE

Lucas

ALL THE REASONS not to do this come flooding in, as if my body chemistry sent them a blanket invitation to invade. My stomach shifts uneasily and I glance in the rearview mirror. Mason is busy playing on his iPod, completely oblivious. Maybe that's a good thing. No reason for him to be upset or nervous about meeting Riley. I've got that covered in spades for the both of us. God, I hope I'm doing this right.

My fingers tighten around the steering wheel, knuckles turning white. "What was I thinking?"

"Dad, how long until we see Uncle Tony?"

Damn kid. Of course he had to bring up the other reason I'm a ball of fucking nerves. "Later this afternoon. But first there's someone I want you to meet."

"Another SEAL?"

Well, not sure what that says about my parenting. I shake my head. "No. Someone who lives with me now. We . . . got married."

Silence.

I look into the rearview mirror once again. Mason's lips downturn and he returns to whatever game he was playing a moment ago. I should've asked Lisa about how to break the news about my relationship status to our son, but talking to my ex-wife about joining the program isn't something I'm ready to do either. Not when I haven't even told my best friend yet that they found a match for me.

"What if she doesn't like me?"

I swallow hard, almost slamming on the brakes. Should've taken Mason out for breakfast and had this talk with him over waffles. Some place I could give him my full attention. "Riley will love you. You're the best kid ever. Well, outside of Tony, of course."

"Dad. He's a grown-up."

"Says you," I say and Mason giggles. Some of the tension in my shoulders dissipates at the gleeful tone in my son's voice. "Anyway, Riley isn't a stranger. I grew up with her. We went to school together."

"Oh." Mason's face contorts, brows furrowed, and he exhales loudly. "Does Mom know?"

"Haven't gotten around to speaking to her yet."

And it won't go over well. Not when Riley was a point of contention during our marriage at times. During some fights, Lisa accused me of being closed off because of the way my high school girlfriend had broken my heart. While some of it may have been true, most of the time I'd just learned to compartmentalize too well because of my job. To shut off emotions because I didn't want to deal with them.

I clear my throat. "Bud, I don't want to stick you in the middle, so can you do me a favor and keep it on the down low for now? Let me tell your mom."

He nods, a tiny smirk on his face. "Your funeral."

Damnit. Should've kept Martinez and my son separated from day one. Never knew personality and sarcasm were contagious and long lasting. But when it comes to Anthony Martinez, who knows what he spreads into this world?

I shake my head. God help Inara and any future kids they have. For sure there will be a lot of parent-teacher conferences due to language and attitude, thanks to their father.

We talk the rest of the car ride home, though it really feels more like a cross-examination with all the questions Mason keeps throwing at me. By the time I pull into the driveway, I think my son knows more about my new wife than he does about me. "Why don't you ever ask me this many questions about myself?"

"Cause you're my dad."

"So?"

Mason shrugs, then tucks his iPod into his pocket as I kill the engine. We both sit in the car, staring at the front door for a few minutes, trying to build up the courage to face the unknown that lies on the other side. After unbuckling my seat belt, I look back over my shoulder. "Ready, bud?"

He nods and squares his little shoulders.

We hop out of the truck and meet at the walk path. Mason holds out his hand and I grab it before we continue toward the house. Once inside, he looks around as if expecting Riley to greet us. Thing is, I didn't tell her I was picking my son up.

Didn't tell her about the barbeque we'd be attending later either. And that she'd be meeting my teammates. I couldn't figure out how. I kept coming up with different scenarios in my head and none of them went well. Then time ran out. Hopefully, she doesn't get mad, but wouldn't blame her if she did. This is all so new, and it's . . . Riley . . . so I'm at a loss about how to act. Still wrapping my head around this whole program and how they assigned my high school girlfriend to be my wife. Talk about a mind fuck.

"Luc, is that . . .?" Riley comes into the main area from the kitchen wearing a pair of stone-gray joggers with a light-blue top, an oversized aqua mug in her hand. Her blond hair is in a messy bun on top of her head, as if she just tumbled out of a well-used bed. God, she looks sexy. I try to say something, but my voice seems stuck in my throat. She glances from me to Mason and smiles. "Um, hi."

After clearing my throat, I place a hand on Mason's shoulder. "Mason, this is Riley. And Riley, this is my son, Mason."

Riley comes closer and extends a hand, which Mason takes into his own. "Nice to meet you, Mason. Your dad told me a bit about you."

"Does your family really own a horse ranch? How many horses do you have? Does it smell like poop?" Mason blurts out.

My eyes widen. So much for worrying about my son being anxious. Seems like informing him about Riley's family has given him something to focus on. Though, quite curious where the poop question came from . . . oh, wait . . . Tony. Gotta be. Sometimes I wonder why I ever allow my teammate to babysit.

Riley kneels down so that she's at eye level with Mason. "Yes, my family has a horse ranch with about twenty horses. Sometimes it does smell like poop, but not in the house. Well, you sort of get used to it, so maybe."

Mason's face scrunches up. "You get used to smelling horse poop?"

Riley chuckles and nods. "Yup. After a while, you don't even notice it." Then she stands up and looks at me with those beautiful blue eyes that I got lost in growing up. I worry that I'll see a storm brewing in them for not telling her about bringing Mason over, but she offers me a smile. "Made some waffles if either of you are interested."

Mason takes off his jacket and hands it to me, then follows Riley toward the kitchen. "Okay, but we shouldn't eat a lot, since we have to go to Bear's house this afternoon."

My new wife stops dead in her tracks and spins around, pinning me with a glare. Apparently throwing in the barbeque is a bridge too far on the surprise front. "Mason, why don't you go take a seat at the table while I talk to your dad for a moment?"

What I wouldn't give to rewind the clock and walk back out the door. Shoving my hands into the pockets of my jeans, I straighten, then start to close the distance between us. Except Riley holds up a hand, palm facing me, and I stop in my tracks. Then she points to the front door. "Outside."

"Excuse me?"

"We need to talk and I'm not doing it in here." She indicates the kitchen with a head nod.

Fair enough. Gotta give her credit for not chewing me out within earshot of my son. Growing up, Riley certainly didn't care which of our friends was around when she read me the riot act, which she did on a couple of occasions. She could have a short fuse. Like her dad.

We step out into the cool April morning. A soft breeze envelopes us, the smell of wet grass filling my nose. No sooner do I turn my eyes skyward when Riley growls. "What were you thinking?"

I turn to face her, but before I could get a word out, she steps closer, poking me in the chest. "You blindsided me. How is this fair?"

Defensiveness wells up in my chest and the best defense is a good offense. I push back instead of backing down. "The paperwork included the fact I had a child, and it was mentioned when you moved in. If it was a problem, you shoulda told the committee."

Her faced turns red. "That's not what I mean. A heads-up would've been nice about both meeting your son and going to Bear's house, whoever that is."

I quirk a brow. "Who said you were invited?"

Her mouth opens and closes, no sound coming out, and

she takes a giant step back. She turns to face the door, then back to me, hand flailing about in the air. "Mason . . . I thought . . ."

While it was cute to rattle my new wife, something I used to do when we were younger as well, there will be hell to pay once she realizes what I'm doing. And that moment just arrived, courtesy of the grin I can't stop from spreading across my face, no matter how hard I try.

"Are you kidding me right now?" She places her hands on her hips. "How do you know I don't already have plans?"

"I don't. And if you do, that's fine. Don't have to come along." Might be easier if she didn't. Breaking the news to everyone is going to be nerve-wracking enough, let alone having her there. And Tony will surely ride her last nerve the way he jokes around. I sigh. I know she's right about how I handled this. "Didn't think this through well enough."

"Tell me something I don't know."

I narrow my eyes. "Try working the hours I do and balancing a new wife and a child."

Riley straightens. "Figured you were just hiding out at work. You've hardly been around for a week and a half. Sort of got used to having the house to myself."

"Hiding? You wish. This is my life. Part of the reason Lisa left in the first place." My throat tightens at the admission. But I refocus my attention, watching my new wife for any tics, any sudden movements. "Why'd you sign up to get married if you were just looking for a roommate?"

And again, not the best move. Riley's face goes from red

to a deep crimson. There might even be smoke coming from her ears, but I'd rather keep my distance than lean in closer to look. Instead of biting my head off, she closes her eyes and takes a few deep breaths. Definitely never expected that.

"Lucas, I'd appreciate it if in the future you inform me about events we need to go to. And a heads-up on when Mason normally comes over as well. Not that I would ever object, but I wouldn't want to be caught walking around the house naked."

My breath catches in my throat as a mental picture begins to form. My dick begins to grow in my jeans. While I certainly noticed Riley's beauty—because it was hard not to—I'd done a decent enough job not picturing her naked. Until now. Now I can't picture anything else. "You walk around the house *naked*?"

She rolls her eyes. "No. But I have darted from the bathroom to my room and vice versa without any clothes on. It takes four steps to go from one to the other." Riley slaps my arm. "You better not be picturing it."

"Kinda hard not to." Our eyes meet and something passes between us, something hot.

Before either of us can say another word, the front door opens. Mason stands in the doorway staring at us. "Can we eat now?"

Riley smiles at him. "Absolutely."

Before she walks off, I grab her wrist. "Listen, you're right. I'll be more forthcoming with the schedule as best as I can. Things come up unexpectedly at work, so can't do much there. And sometimes with Mason as well. Part of being a parent. I'll do what I can, though."

"Thank you." She quirks a brow at me. "Is your friend's name really Bear?"

I chuckle. Mostly because when anyone meets the burly, redheaded giant who looks like a Special Forces terminator, the last thing expected would be that his name is Henry. "No, it's a nickname. But it's what everyone calls him. Even his wife. Well, unless he's in deep shit."

"Gotcha."

The three of us sit around the table, eating, and answering all the questions Mason throws out. I sit back and take a swig of my lukewarm coffee, watching Riley and my son interact. She's a natural with kids. And the way she thought about stepping outside to argue, then recentering herself when she got angry . . . she certainly has changed from the teenage girl I'd known.

And loved.

Shit. Can't go there. Won't go there. She left me once already, and just because she's good with my kid doesn't mean anything. She could easily walk right back out the door tomorrow. Doesn't matter she gave me her word, especially not if deep down inside, she believes what her father told her all those years ago, that I would never be able to take care of her.

Granted, I'm a long way from the poor kid I was growing up. I know firsthand how money doesn't buy love and passion, something Riley probably doesn't understand since she never had to suffer in any way growing up in the big mansion her family owned. What hardship has she ever known?

Then the vision of that studio apartment I picked her up from floats through my mind. Something still doesn't add up there. I'll figure it out eventually, though.

MAYBE I SHOULDN'T have had two cups of coffee. Certainly isn't helping with my nerves. I scan the driveway and the area in front of Bear's house as we pull up to the curb, a sense of relief flooding me that Tony's car isn't there. How I want to kick myself for feeling this way, but I need some extra time to prepare. My best friend certainly isn't going to make this meeting go well. He's a notorious jokester and he also knows my history with Riley, stories shared during those ominous moments during war when we welcomed any reprieve, even if it meant talking about our broken hearts.

"Don't see Uncle Tony's car," Mason called out from the back seat. "You sure he's back from the officer training school?"

"Yes. And it's Officer Candidate School."

Mason shrugs me off and goes back to scoping the street for my best friend's truck.

Riley fidgets with her purse, a forced smile on her face. "So, are you close with all your teammates? Or just some of them?"

The question catches me by surprise. Most know how bonded the guys in teams were, but I forget Riley doesn't know much about the life. "We're like family. Been through a lot together. One of us even died a couple of deployments ago. Families are all close too."

"Oh. Sorry for your loss." She looks stricken.

I park the truck and we all hop out like a family. The feeling is odd. Even Mason hangs back with us instead of running off into Bear's house. The front door is open, so we all walk inside and follow the voices to the kitchen.

"Craiger, nice of you to make it. Want a beer?" Bear holds out an amber bottle, all smiles until his eyes fall onto the woman standing behind me. Then his eyes shoot to mine, brows furrowed.

It's not like I haven't brought a date to one of our gatherings before, but never when Mason's there. I scratch the back of my head and glance around the room. Trevor Graves—the newest member of the team and one of the youngest, and possibly a mite too pretty for everyone to feel settled around him—and Jim Stephens are staring, bodies completely still.

"Uh, this is Riley. My wife."

Stephens chokes on whatever he was trying to swallow. Graves looks around the room as he forces back a smile. Bear blinks rapidly as if I were his eldest daughter informing her burly father I'd just eloped in Vegas.

"Oh my God. Did I just hear you correctly?" Marge walks in from another room, followed by Taya. "When did you get married?"

Taya tilts her head, gaze bouncing from me to Riley to Stephens, her husband. "Wait. Did you join the program? Is this another match?"

"Yes, Lucas and I were assigned to one another. We're not strangers, though. We grew up together in Texas." Riley steps around me and walks over to the women.

They all start talking while my friends remain tight-lipped. All except Graves. "Martinez know?"

I shake my head.

"Can't wait for them to meet," he says.

"Me too." Mason high-fives the newest member of our team.

"Can't wait for me to meet who?"

We spin around to find Tony and his wife, Inara, another couple brought together by the military's spouse-matching program, standing in the entranceway to the kitchen. Fuck. My palms start to sweat. I'm not ready for this.

"Hola, missed everyone." Inara scoots around her husband and runs over to Mason and gives him a hug, before hurrying over to the rest of the wives, eyes locked on Riley.

"¡Cuánto tiempo sin verlo!" Martinez wraps me in a big hug and thumps me hard on the back. "Who's the blonde?"

Bear sets his drink down with a *thunk*. "Supposedly, his new wife."

Martinez looks over my shoulder to where my wife stands. "¡Bien hecho! What's her name?"

"Riley. Her and Dad grew up together." After Mason throws me under the bus, he runs over and leaps into

Martinez's arms.

A chair scrapes against the floor and coughing fills the air. Everyone stops and turns to find Stephens pounding a fist on his own chest, face turning red and eyes watering. Taya runs over and pats him on the back while the rest of the group gathers in.

Meanwhile, my son is giving Martinez the biggest hug he can muster. "Missed you, Uncle Tony. Happy birthday again. Sorry we didn't get to have cake together last month."

"Missed you too, buddy. And don't worry, I'm sure Mrs. Donaghue will whip up one of her yummy creations."

He's referring to Marge, who narrows her eyes at him, most likely as a warning not to take her for granted. But none of us do. The fiery, petite redhead does so much for all of us. Which includes being the birthday cake baker.

When Martinez finally lowers Mason, he turns to my wife and extends his hand. "You're the infamous Riley. Encantada de conocerte. Heard so much about you. And here I thought coming home itself would be the best birthday present."

Riley shakes his hand. "Expected more from you the way Mason carried on about his uncle being so funny."

Martinez places both hands over his heart and balks.

I pinch the bridge of my nose. "Please don't get him started."

"Pendejo, you didn't even tell me you signed up for the program." Martinez shook his head. "What else have I missed? Well, besides meeting Stephens's kid. Where is the little bugger?"

"Sleeping upstairs." Jim folds his arms across his chest. "And don't go waking him."

I forgot. Riley wasn't the only person Inara and Martinez were going to meet today. The newest—youngest—member of our family is here. I shake my head. Seems like ages ago Taya and Stephens met. Through the same program, no less. They were one of the first couples matched. Then we almost lost Taya when some psycho tried to kill her. But look at them now. A happy family, complete with a new baby. Inara and Martinez are happy together too.

Maybe the committee saw something Riley and I both missed. The success rate of the program so far is pretty high. About eighty-seven percent. They must know something about what they're doing. My gaze falls to Riley, blond hair in a high ponytail, talking animatedly to Inara and Taya and Marge. She tilts her head back to laugh and something in my chest unfurls a tiny bit.

Maybe, just maybe, this marriage might work out.

CHAPTER SIX

Riley

MASON AND HIS friend are in the living room playing video games. I never knew watching kids could be so easy. The two boys didn't argue, came to eat, scarfed the food down without a word, then rushed back off to continue playing. Maybe video games aren't so bad. They are definitely making my first day with Mason alone much easier.

And they didn't require me to change my wardrobe. I lean a hand on the counter and take a second to close my eyes. Blech. Nausea. Not a lot. Just a little. Just enough to make me feel slightly off-kilter. Which is why I'm still wearing my Sexy Kitten pajamas. Not that I feel sexy. They were supposed to lift my spirits when I got them. So, when I'm not one hundred percent, I sport the solid black top with sultry cat eyes made of silver glitter and matching velvet shorts that have *Sexy Kitten* written all over them.

They're also my go-to for whenever the sad truth that I haven't had sex in over five years comes floating to the front of my mind. My celibacy started because of my health. Not to mention the one guy I dated in college walked out on me during a flare-up as if he couldn't be bothered. Then I moved back home to my parents' house, although I'm not sure it would have been any better anywhere else. It was hard to be sick and fight to make it on my own, and be sexy all at the same time. In fact, it was impossible.

Which also happens to be why I haven't mentioned anything to Lucas yet about my condition. Luckily no one really questioned why I didn't eat much at his friend's barbeque and he hasn't said anything the few times we've eaten together. I just want a chance to build a solid relationship with someone who doesn't know about my disease. To see if such a thing is even possible. Not that Lucas is my forever or anything. He's temporary. But what better way to experiment and see if people do exist who can give me a chance to prove myself as capable before they prejudge?

Also, a premade family is perfect. While I would love to have kids of my own, all the surgeries, along with the Crohn's, make it too risky. So, marrying a man with a child is a way to safely fulfill that need that still aches in my heart. Mason gives me the opportunity to practice being a stepmom. Maybe more than practice. Maybe really be that stepmom. Except that would mean staying married to Lucas and that wouldn't be fair to him. "Besides, how am I going to become the new version of myself that I desperately want to be when I'm literally married to my past?"

That is the fifty-million-dollar question.

With a sigh I drop down into the chair at the kitchen table and stare out the window. Lucas has been great so far when he's been home. We're developing a friendship built on respect and admiration. But again, he isn't exactly the fresh start I'd hoped for.

I reach into my purse and take out my wallet. Inside, tucked behind my license, is the very first love letter Lucas ever wrote me. He was such a romantic. Come to think about it, he expressed himself better in his letters than he ever did in words. Though I never minded. There was something exciting about finding a letter hidden in my locker or one that had been stuffed into my backpack when I wasn't looking.

I unfold the letter and read through it, the pencil fading but the words still readable. How simple those days had been. Brighter and full of hope as well.

Dearest Riley,

This morning when I saw you walking up to my locker, I thought my heart was going to burst. The best part of every one of my days is when you smile at me and this morning your smile was even more dazzling than usual. It's like all your goodness, your kindness, your bravery, your strength was shining from you and it was all directed at me. I don't think I've ever felt luckier.

But then you took my hand in yours and then that was the luckiest I've ever felt.

From the first time I saw you, walking into school our freshman year, you made my heart beat faster. I know now, though, that was shallow. That was all about how beautiful you are. It was about your shining blond hair, your clear blue eyes, your cute little butt. It was about the outside beautifulness of you.

Now I know about the inside beauty of you too. I know how much of you that you give to others. I know how you'll take time to bottle-feed a little lamb who has no mama. I know you'll stop to give a hand-up to someone on the other team who's fallen during a soccer match. I know you never let anything stop you or stand in your way. I know how you look out at the ocean, and instead of seeing danger, you see adventure and opportunity. From the time you jumped on that wild mare to when you backtalk your father whenever he has something to say about the trailer park I live in, you've shown yourself to be one of the strongest and most fearless people I know.

I liked you the second I saw you and my feelings are growing stronger and stronger every day. Every new thing I learn about you makes my love grow. Sometimes I don't think I can love you more, but then you do something brave and smart and kind, and I do.

You are my sun and my moon, Riley.

Love,
Lucas

The letter pointed out everything Lucas liked about me, things my family had seemed to forget because my illness overshadowed the rest. That's part of the reason I'd always kept the letter in my wallet. For days when I feel less than, for those hard days when I need to wear my sexy kitten pajamas, I can remember the girl I used to be and the woman I hope to become. Maybe I could even become that woman with him by my side. Maybe we could have the life we could have had if I hadn't gotten sick and sent him away.

If only I could trust Lucas would see the same girl instead of the sick one like everyone else always does once they find out about my battles with Crohn's.

My thumb grazes over the soft loose-leaf paper. I should really make a photocopy before it falls completely apart. After refolding it, I place it back into my wallet, which I then put back in my purse.

I grab the bowl of honey-flavored pretzel twists, leave the kitchen, and head down the stairs into the family room. "You boys still playing?"

Mason turns his head toward me. "Yea, do you want to play?"

I plop down onto the suede sectional couch and bite into a pretzel as I stare at the screen. "Would love to. But what kind of game is this? Soccer with . . . cars?"

"Yeah. Here, take the controller. I'll show you how to play." Mason jumps to his feet and is at my side.

"She can just do the tutorials," Parker says.

Mason shrugs, presses a bunch of buttons, then hands me the controller. On the screen is some sort of blue race car with flames coming out of the back. Mason and Parker sit on either side. Mason points at the buttons on the top corner of the controller. "One is RB and the other is LB. If you follow what the screen says, it will tell you how to shoot the ball and move around."

"Get the yellow balls. Those are for boosting. It helps you go faster," Parker points out as I drive my virtual car toward a giant soccer ball.

I miss and laugh. "This is harder than it looks."

"You get used to it. Takes practice. Mason gets stuck driving up the wall sometimes."

After a few attempts and more laughs, I hand the controller back. "You know what? Why don't you two play and I'll watch? It'll give me time to understand the game and maybe next time I can join in."

"You don't have to wait until I come to visit. I have the game at my mom's house too. We can connect online and play," Mason says.

I swallow the pretzel I'd been chewing. Weird . . . why would he want to play with me? "I'm sure I don't measure up to your other friends. You'd probably get bored."

"He doesn't have friends where his mom lives," Parker says.

Mason lets out a deep growl then turns to face his friend. "Shut up, dummy."

"Hey, boys. That's not the way to talk to one another. And what does Parker mean, you don't have any friends?" I place the bowl down on the coffee table in front of us and angle myself to face Mason.

He avoids my gaze, concentrating on the game. "Parker

doesn't know what he's talking about."

"Uh, yeah, I do. You FaceTime all of us every day talking about how your school sucks and how you hate it. You even said you wished your dad got hurt so he could stay home more and you could move back here."

My breath catches at Parker's words. Mason had actually wished his father to get hurt. To stay home. I take a deep, centering breath. I'm not really sure what my place is in this situation, but Lucas had mentioned his son was having a hard time. Maybe I can find a little more information out to help. "Mason, do you really not like your other school?"

Mason lets his car crash in the game. His shoulders hunch inward, so tense that they quiver. "The other kids, they don't understand. Their parents aren't gone like mine and Parker's dads. They're not in the military, and when I say my dad is on a mission, they say I'm lying and my dad left because he didn't want me."

My heart beats so hard, I'm afraid it might come out of my chest. Sadness and rage war within me. Is it wrong for a twenty-nine-year-old woman to want to beat the crap out of some snot-nosed children? A growl deep within my chest rumbles as I recall how mean some kids were back in high school. How they'd make fun of Lucas for the clothes he wore and point out his family's financial status.

"Did you tell your teachers?" I do my best to keep my voice steady. No sense is showing how riled up I am as it won't help Mason.

Both boys turn and stare at me as if I'd just unplugged

their game. With a groan, Mason shakes his head. "Tattling will make it worse. Then I'll be a rat *and* a kid whose dad doesn't like him. It was better here where the other kids understood what it's like. A lot of the kids here have parents like mine. Sometimes our moms and dads went away together. Sometimes they went different places. Those kids know what it's like, about how our parents love us and aren't running away, even if they have to go away."

My heart keeps breaking listening to Mason, my gaze bouncing between both boys. This is the life they live, knowing their fathers might not come home. But they both seem to know they are loved. They are so brave. Whatever Mason needs from me, I vow to be there for him. The more people on his side, the better. "I'll talk to your dad about it. We'll figure out a way to help."

Mason jumps up. "No!"

I pull back, blinking. Not the reaction I expected. Well, not the harshness of it.

"You've gotta promise, Riley. You can't tell Dad." He wrings his hands. "I can take care of it myself."

"Why, Mason? Maybe he can help." I reach out to take his hands and still them.

"He can't." He shakes his head. "He'll only worry, and if he's worried, he'll get distracted, and if he gets distracted . . ." His words fade out.

My gaze turns to Parker who has also become sullen. The image of the kids at the Gold Star Family Surf School comes back to me. If Lucas is distracted at his job, he might not come home. "I get it, Mason."

"Then you won't tell him?" he says, looking up at me with eyes that are just a bit too shiny. He holds up his hand, crooked pinkie forward. "Pinkie-swear?"

I curl my little finger around his. "Pinkie-swear."

Mason nods and sits back down. "I'll talk to Mom. I promise. Just please don't make my dad worry."

"Okay, but be sure you talk to your mom about it, okay?" Uneasy, I grab my laptop and research online jobs as the boys return to playing their video game, laughing and poking at each other as if the conversation we just had never happened. But whether or not I should say something to Lucas keeps nagging at me. Nothing like feeling caught in the middle, and being the new person in the family, I'm not sure what to do. Hopefully, Mason will talk to his mother and she'll relay the information to my husband.

I shake myself and refocus on my own situation. I need a job that can accommodate my Crohn's flare-ups and has benefits that will help cover the medications and treatments I need. It's all fine and well to have Lucas's insurance now, but being able to take care of myself is a necessity because there is no guarantee at the end of the year Lucas will continue to want to be married. That was never my intention anyway. This marriage, this assignment, is only supposed to be temporary. A holdover until I can do things on my own. The fact that it's Lucas doesn't change anything. Or so I keep telling myself. Because I can't seem to stop thinking about what it might be like if we were really together.

Speaking of taking care of myself, I should be hearing back soon about my qualifications for the new medication. Shame how long it takes. But at least the place has financial assistance since the drugs are new and no one's insurance will cover them yet.

I scroll through a couple of websites that list work-from-home jobs that offer medical benefits and click open tabs to a couple of companies that catch my eye. Most offer minimum wage but the bonuses like paid training and retirement benefits are definitely a plus.

Just as I complete the seventh application, the doorbell rings. After closing my laptop and placing it on the coffee table, I stand and make my way up the stairs to the front door. The boys are supposed to be here for another hour or so before Lucas gets home to drive them back to their respective households, and I'm not expecting anyone. Maybe my husband ordered something in the mail? I hope it's not someone selling something.

When I pull open the door, I'm met with a woman who is about my height. She looks a bit more athletic than I am, wearing skinny jeans and a red silk shirt. Her black hair cascades over her shoulders, sunglasses sitting on top of her head. The woman's eyes go wide as she takes me in, her mouth pinching together.

Her picture didn't do her justice.

I tuck a strand of hair behind my ears before hugging myself and wishing I'd gotten dressed. Ugh, definitely don't feel like a sexy kitten compared to Lucas's ex-wife. She's gorgeous and glamorous. And this is definitely not the first impression I intended to make. "Hi."

"I'm Mason's mother. Is Lucas home? He should have told me if he couldn't watch the boys. I would have been here sooner. He didn't need to hire a babysitter. Kinda defeats the damn purpose of spending time with his son." The woman sucks in a breath and places her fingertips to her lips. "I'm so sorry. Didn't mean to offend you. It's just my son was looking forward to spending time with his father."

Biting my lip, I scratch the side of my head. Babysitter? Oh, maybe she'd never seen a picture of me. And the way I'm dressed, I could see why she might think that. Could this be any more awkward? "Actually, I'm Lucas's wife. Sorry, I wasn't expecting you. Lucas got a call that he had to go to the base right after he brought the boys over, but he said he'd be back in time to drive them home."

The woman stares, unblinking. Then a myriad of expressions crosses her face. Oh, crap. She doesn't know. Seriously, freaking awkward. And why the hell didn't Lucas talk to her? I mean, how didn't she know? Mason surely would have said something, wouldn't he? Unless my husband told his son not to mention it.

Was I some dirty little secret? No. That doesn't make sense. Two of his friends went through the same program, so there wasn't anything to be ashamed of. Yet, he didn't tell them at first and he clearly didn't tell his ex. I have no idea how to explain it to a former spouse as I have never been married. Why on earth hasn't he told her?

I clear my throat, hoping to break the trance Mason's mom appears to be stuck in. "Do you want me to go get the boys for you? Are you taking Parker home too?"

"Oh, um, yes. That would be great. And my name is Lisa."

"Riley." I push the storm door open so Lisa can come inside. "I'll be right back."

When the boys and I return, Lisa has their jackets ready and appears to be in a rush. Her tone is clipped with every answer she offers her son, and she is almost shoving him into his jacket, yet occasionally looking at me as if trying to get as far away from me as possible.

Not sure what I expected, but this wasn't it.

Okay, time to try to clear some of the tension. "The boys had lunch and we had some pretzels. They were well-behaved and played video games."

"I'm sure they did."

I'd have to be halfway across the world to miss the sarcastic tone she answered in. What was this woman's problem? I step forward. "Did I do something to offend you?"

"No, we're just in a rush." Lisa ushers the boys out the door, both Parker and Mason stopping for a second to turn and wave bye.

Once they are in the car and Lisa pulls out of the driveway, I shut the front door and lean against it. Well, that . . . wasn't fun. Maybe she felt threatened?

But how am I supposed to act? What am I supposed to do? One thing's for sure. The program didn't prepare me for how to handle an ex-wife who was the mother of my spouse's son and hadn't been told that I even existed.

Maybe signing up for this program wasn't such a great idea.

CHAPTER SEVEN

Lucas

"YOU'RE MARRIED?" LISA'S voice booms into the truck. "When the hell did that happen, Lucas?"

"Uh . . ." I can't quite get words to form. I look over at Bear in the passenger seat, who has closed his eyes and is shaking his giant head.

"Lucas?" Lisa prompts.

"Almost two weeks ago," I manage to say, but she's not really listening.

"You realize I showed up to pick up Mason and spoke to her like she was the babysitter."

"Why were you picking up Mason anyway? I was going to take him and Parker home. That's what we agreed on. Planned on having the whole 'I'm married' conversation when I got to your house. Today's the first day our schedules actually lined up and it wasn't news I felt was appropriate to text. A face-to-face was the most respectful way to tell you." If she'd stuck to the plan, none of this would have happened.

"I was trying to do you a favor by not making you drive all the way over to my new place."

Helluva favor. "Well, you shoulda told me instead of just showing up."

"Lucas, do you really think that that's the issue here? That I picked up Mason instead of waiting for you to bring him home?"

I latch on to the steering wheel, my knuckles turning white. Why did Lisa have to change the schedule without updating me? It was my job to inform my ex-wife I'd remarried. Not Riley's. But damn if anything ever goes my way.

"And I take it Mason knew already which means you told him to keep something from me. Do you not see that as a problem? And Riley? Is this the same Riley, the girl from high school who dropped you like an old pair of shoes that went out of style?" Lisa's voice rose in pitch with each word.

Bear remained quiet and stared out the window. He'd always liked Lisa. Most of the team did. She was normally easygoing. They'd all understood when she'd asked for a divorce. It was part of our lives. Marriages tended to fail. But we all remained friends. She was even at Jim's wedding with her now fiancé.

"Lisa, I barely had time to talk to the guys about it." I let out a long breath. "And it's not like I got to choose who I was assigned to. A committee made the choice."

"Why did you even sign up for some stupid program like that?"

"Because it worked for Jim and for Tony. I thought it might work for me. What? I can't be happy? Find someone who can handle my life?" I wanted to kick myself the moment the words left my mouth.

For the first time during our twenty-minute drive, Bear turned toward me, his eyes narrowed to mere slits. I swear in that moment, he might as well have been Lisa's father with the way he appeared to want to beat the shit out of me. Not that I blame him. That last part was a low blow.

"I'm sorry, Lisa. I didn't mean—"

"Lucas, I get it. The life is hard, and you wanted someone this time who could handle it. But Riley? After everything you told me, after everything you shared with me about how she made you feel?"

"Lisa, it's honestly none of your business."

"Except my son visits your home. And you left her alone with him. What if she flaked out with him? That is not happening on my watch."

I grind my molars. Lisa is overreacting. Nothing had happened. There was eating and video game playing, and not some inappropriate game either. Leaving Mason with Riley is far better than leaving him with Martinez. Yet, Lisa has never minded when my best friend had watched our son. Not even when Mason came home asking if girls in real life danced in their underwear on a table, thanks to some stupid movie he'd watched with Martinez.

"I got a lawyer. With the move and me getting married, I wasn't sure if there'd be any issues. But things have changed, and I want full custody of Mason." Lisa's words echo through the car.

My heart stops and I can't suck any air into my lungs. Luckily, we had just arrived at Bear's house and I pulled the car over, throwing it into "park" because the darkness at the corner of my eyes is growing larger. "What the fuck did you just say?"

"I said I am going to push for full custody of our son."

"Why? Because I married Riley? You don't get to approve who I marry. I certainly didn't give you any shit when you started dating or when you got engaged. Or even when you decided to move the fuck away."

"Lucas, I am all of thirty minutes from you. And Riley isn't Mason's parent. You are. What is the point of him being there if you are going to be at work and she's babysitting him? You're the one he wants the relationship with."

I turn to Bear, who sits quietly in the seat. He could have already gotten out. But we are brothers, there to support one another through thick and thin. Plus, he has two daughters. He's who I turn to when I question whether or not I'm a good father. Or when I become afraid that my job might ruin my child. Which is way more often than I'd like.

I swallow past the freaking large lump in my throat. "Fine. Well, looks like I'll be hiring a lawyer too."

I disconnect the call before Lisa can say another word.

Bear grunts. "Shit's going to get ugly, brotha. I'm here for you. But one thing. She's right. Mason needs you to be there when you can. Don't force Riley on him. Won't turn out good for anyone."

I nod because I have no words. I'd just gotten blindsided

like a hapless quarterback who'd been taken down hard by Lawrence Taylor. Bear pats my shoulder and exits my truck. I take a few minutes after he leaves to collect myself. My heart races, the pressure in my neck and temples grows. Great. All I need now is to let the stress get so out of control that I have a heart attack.

Burning rage hisses through my body like deathly poison, screeching a demanded release. Like a volcano erupting, the wrath sweeps off me in ferocious waves. But I'm in my truck and the only outlet I have is slamming my steering wheel over and over.

Never in a million years did I think marrying my high school sweetheart would lead my ex-wife to try to take my son away from me. After everything we went through. After the gunshot wounds, our friend dying, other funerals. After all of it, Lisa never once mentioned Mason was better off without me.

"How things fucking change." The words have the maximum amount of vitriol I can expend.

By the time I get home, my anger hasn't abated. Instead, anxiety joins the damn party because now I have to find a lawyer and I have no idea where to even begin. What if I hire someone inept? This fucking day needs to be over.

I walk into the house through the garage entrance and find Riley all curled up on the couch in pajama pants and cozy socks, watching TV. My hand tightens around the door handle and my anger becomes impossible to keep at bay. "Is this what you did all day? Did you just ignore my son to watch TV?"

Riley sits up, eyes blinking. She even looks a bit pale, like she had the day we moved her out of the apartment she'd been living in. Her eyes narrow, but then she just leans back into the couch as if she doesn't have the energy to say what is really on her mind. "We had lunch. We talked. Mason and Parker even attempted to show me how to play their video game."

I shove the door closed. Hard. Then kick off my boots and stalk into the room. "Then why is Lisa pushing for full custody?"

"I'm so sorry, Luc." She frowns. "It might have helped if she'd known I was here and we got married. Can't imagine what it was like for her to show up and find me."

She's right. No way around that. I pace back and forth. I rake my hands through my hair, nails digging into my scalp. "Fuck my life."

"We'll get through this. Mason adores you. You should see how his face lights up when he talks about you."

I close my eyes and when I open them, I turn to Riley. Hell. Pale didn't describe her color. It's worse than that. She doesn't look well at all. And here I am unloading on her for a situation I created. I take a few steps toward the couch and sit. "Are you okay?"

Riley's gaze shifts from me back to the TV show.

"Riley, are you okay?"

She looks at the pillow and lies back down, curling into a ball. "Yeah, just something I ate. Anyway, don't you have a custody agreement with Lisa?"

I hesitate for a moment. Riley's trying to divert. Or at least minimizing how she feels for my sake. I study her for another moment, the way she hugs her stomach slightly, the tightening of her jaw. Well, she's definitely having some stomach issues. Maybe I'll make her some soup later.

"Lucas?"

I clear my throat. "No. We never had anything official. After she moved out, she didn't live far. Only five minutes away. Mason remained in the same school, had the same friends. But then she started dating and when she got engaged, she moved, and moved Mason with her."

"So, she hired a lawyer today? Because of me?"

I shake my head. "Appears she had one."

Riley blows out a loud breath. "Maybe she's been looking to get full custody for a while. Could be because of her soon-to-be husband."

"Full custody isn't an option for me. Not with my job." I drop by head back onto the couch and stare at the ceiling. I joined the program hoping it would work, hoping marrying Riley would somehow help my son. Instead, it might wreck it all. "Maybe I should talk to the committee about annulling the marriage and dropping out of the program."

Riley goes very still. "I don't think you getting married is the issue."

I groan. "You're probably right. Lisa was always complaining about my job constantly getting in the way when it came to Mason, so maybe I'm just screwed either way.

Today just being another example."

Riley shifts and leans the throw pillow against my leg, then rests her head on it. "It'll work out. Maybe she's just upset you didn't give her the heads-up. With Mason having a hard time, she might be concerned another change might not be good for him. Talk to her."

She could be right. Riley hasn't had the opportunity to show Lisa that she can be a positive in Mason's life. And if my wife is this under the weather and still managed to take care of both Mason and Parker, there is nothing for Lisa to fear. They all need time to get used to one another.

Riley looks up at me. "Lucas, look, we are exes. We had a relationship years ago and there's no reason we couldn't work on rebuilding that bond, which, in turn, will help Mason feel more secure. We just have to convince Lisa the program works, and we offer a great home for your son."

"I'll hold off on talking to the committee. Let me get a lawyer first and see what they say." I brush her hair back. Her skin feels warm to the touch, and I bend over to place a soft kiss on her cheek. "Thank you."

Maybe she's right about everything. Rekindling love isn't unheard of. It's been done before. And it would be nice for everything to work out in the end. The way it should have the first time.

Maybe fate really is giving us a second chance.

CHAPTER EIGHT

Riley

STALLS, BOOTHS, AND various rides fill the giant grassy field. Some people wander around, popcorn or skewered meat in hand, as they play carnival games such as balloon pops, ring toss, and racing games. Others stand in long lines for rides. Lucas, however, remains quiet by my side, walking in a daze. I'd talked him into coming to the carnival, thinking it might take his mind off his troubles. Instead, it seems to have made him sink deeper into his funk.

I take his hand in mine. "What did the lawyer say?"

Lucas sighs heavily, his shoulders slumping. "Was an introductory meeting. Courts tend to side with the mother, and while he will try to get me a fair visitation schedule, if Lisa wants to follow it verbatim, there won't be much I can do about it. With my job, she'd most likely get full custody. Not that it would be any different than what she unofficially has now."

I chew the inside of my cheek, brows furrowed. So what really is changing then? "Is it the visitation that bothers you? Do you think she wouldn't be flexible?"

He rakes his fingers through his blond hair. "She seemed really pissed. Never seen her like this. But with my job, if she isn't flexible, I'm worried I won't get to see Mason at all."

I squeeze his hand. "All we can do is the best we can with what we can control." That was one of the lessons I'd learned from being sick—to focus on what I can do, not what I wish I could do.

A couple of small children run past us carrying oversized stuffed animals, their faces painted with various designs. Ahead of us is a big canvas tent, the familiar smell of livestock emanating from within it. Most likely a petting zoo.

Lucas tugs me toward the row of food trailers to the left. Everything from chocolate-covered bacon to corn dogs to fried Oreos is being sold. All things I can't or shouldn't eat. Lucas stops at one of the carts. "Can I get two funnel cakes?"

I bite my lip and glance around to see the menu. There's something I can eat. Thank God. "Actually, I'll just take an unsalted pretzel."

Lucas turns to me, eyebrow quirked. "Really?"

I wave a dismissive hand in the air. "Yeah, they never taste as good elsewhere as they do at a carnival. Even when I've gotten the frozen ones at the supermarket, they never come out right. And I've been craving one."

"Okay, then. I'll take one funnel cake and one pretzel." Lucas pays and after we receive our food, we head over to some hay bales next to the ring toss and sit.

Above our heads some loose balloons float away into the darkening sky. Lucas takes a bite of his dessert and appears to be calming down. I nudge him playfully with my shoulder. "Glad you agreed to come out."

"Thanks for the suggestion." His smile is soft and not forced, almost reminiscent of the shy boy I once knew.

I bite into the warm dough of my pretzel and chew as we take in the sights and sounds. There's something special about the aromatic mix of fresh cotton candy and motor oil. Something that can only be found at a carnival. And the hum of the engines running the various trucks and rides is soothing.

Lucas nudges me and points at the Fun House. "Wanna go?"

I snort, my eyes focused on the bored attendant taking tickets at the entrance. "Sure. Beats sitting on the scratchy hay bale."

"Thought you'd be used to that."

"It's not like I'm wearing a sturdy pair of jeans like I would be if I was back home on the ranch." Instead, I'm wearing black yoga pants with pocketed sides, a bright-yellow blouse with embellished swirls around the neckline, and a pair of Chucks. None of which protects me from prodding hay.

We finish our food and then head over to the haunted house. The place is packed. Lucas and I weave through the crowd. Someone bumps into me and I grab Lucas's bicep to regain my balance.

Holy crap.

Lucas was always fit, but I don't remember his arms feeling so solid. I swallow hard, my fingers curling around the vast muscle. He pulls me close and my heart begins to beat faster, body growing warmer. I look up momentarily as he glances down. His eyes are dilated and filled with a recognizable heat. I gulp and avert my gaze, almost thankful for the creepy clown laughter coming from the speakers.

Total mood killer. So's the monster mouth opening we have to walk through. I peer into the darkness in front of us.

Lucas gives the attendant the tickets and I grab his hand as we enter. He looks down, then back at me. "Since when are you scared, Cupcake?"

"Hello . . . don't you remember the haunted house we went to our sophomore year? You had to pick me up and carry me out." I'm not one for being scared in the first place. I don't like horror movies or scary books. But the fire department that sponsored the attraction went all out. We'd heard it was the best and all the proceeds were going to charity. Plus, everybody was going. I'd strolled in thinking it would all be good fun, but then a guy in a hockey mask jumped out from behind a curtain waving an axe, and I'd started screaming and couldn't stop.

"Oh, yeah. How could I forget that? Had to throw you over my shoulder and double-time it out of there." Lucas laughs and laces his fingers through mine. My heart stutters at the sensation and I find it hard to swallow. I can't how much I missed his touch.

A couple of laughing teens push past us and I collide into Lucas. He wraps his arm around me to steady me, and his solid body ignites my nerve endings. While his smell and the cadence of his voice are familiar, the way he has changed physically is new. And exciting.

Ugh. Maybe it's just that I haven't gotten laid in like . . . forever.

"What are you thinking about?" he asks.

I clear my throat and step away. "Just remembering old times."

His brow quirks, a lopsided smile forming on his lips. "Oh, yeah?"

I smack his shoulder. "Not like that."

Totally like that.

We both chuckle and continue on. Of course the theme of the attraction happens to be creepy clowns. Like super creepy. Complete with recorded laughter like I heard outside. Only the dark, cramped space heightens the fear factor. My mouth goes dry and my pulse begins to race. "Maybe this wasn't the best idea. Should've opted for the Ferris wheel."

"We can go there next if you want." He smiles down at me.

I nod, trying to be brave, but feel my lower lip tremble. Suddenly, Lucas is pulling me through the fun house as if trying to get us out of there like his life depended on it. Not that I mind. Definitely didn't need a repeat performance of sophomore year. Then again, my hunky husband tossing me over his shoulder would be kinda hot.

Ugh. Why do I keep going there? I'm happy that we're

friends, but I'm not sure I can chance anything more. There'd be no way to keep my Crohn's a secret, and once that's out, well, forget about it.

We blow through the exit and are climbing into the chair for the Ferris wheel fifteen minutes later. Lucas hasn't released my hand, nor do I want him to. I don't mind the sideways glances either. Or how close he stands to me.

He helps me in and the attendant secures the metal bar. We begin to climb and the sight is amazing. "The moon is so bright."

"Um-hum."

Below us, throngs of people move around, and I can't believe how many are actually here. Crowded is an overstatement. Lucas extends his arm over the back of our seat and I scooch in closer, resting my head on his chest. It feels like it belongs there, like the most natural thing in the world.

His heart is thudding fast.

Neither of us says a word and we just take in the moment. I'm filled with both excitement and anticipation and a whole hell of a lot of nerves. I expected to be attracted to my husband. Hell, we were super passionate when we dated. But I didn't think he'd feel that way about me. Not after the way I just let our relationship go, and didn't bother to contradict my father when he said Lucas wasn't good enough for me.

But it appears I'm wrong.

When I look up, he meets my gaze and holds it, inching his lips closer to mine. Lips I miss. They seem to be one of the few things about him that haven't changed, and I want to get lost in them. I know I shouldn't. I know it's opening a door I might not be able to close. I say it anyway. "Kiss me?"

And he does. Softly.

Too soft, almost as if he's afraid.

His hand rests below my ear, his thumb caressing my cheek as he deepens the kiss. I reach up and grab his head, pulling him closer, my tongue dancing with his. God, how I missed this. How I missed him.

But then everything comes to a screeching halt. And not because of the ride.

My body tenses as his fingers dip below the hem of my shirt. No, I'm not ready for him to discover the rough skin from my scars. Or explain to him how I ended up with both a colostomy and ileostomy bag for a while after one of my surgeries. Or how I had my intestines resected.

Not yet anyway.

So, I break our kiss and pull away. "Luc, I'm not sure we should go any further than kissing."

"Sorry, I didn't mean . . . shit." He leans back. "Didn't want to make you feel uncomfortable."

The hurt in his eyes twists my heart. It's familiar. Not as deep as the day I broke his heart, but still recognizable. Time to ease the tension. "Don't apologize. We have history. It's familiar. I just don't want to jump into anything."

He laughs. "Yeah, we aren't teenagers anymore, even if we were just making out like them."

I rest my head against his shoulder and can't help but smile. Truly smile. Maybe people do get second chances.

CHAPTER NINE

Lucas

THE BEACH IS quieter than normal; only a few joggers and swimmers are here. Seaweed rolls in the surf as white caps slap against the shore. It's not too hot and the cool breeze is refreshing. My wife is walking along beside me holding my hand. Perfect day for the beach. Perfect day for yoga.

I can't believe we've been married almost a month now. Time sure does fly by, and work doesn't seem to help. But I'm doing the best I can and so far Riley seems to be adapting well. Then again, unlike Texas, she doesn't have to travel far to hit the waves to surf. And my wife seems to make it to the beach at least once a week, gauging by the sand she tends to leave behind in the garage.

"It's been so long since I've done any poses. Your mom would be so upset." Riley walks into the water a little way, flinching when her feet hit the cold water.

I laugh and the few seagulls in the area begin squawking as if joining in. Riley pouts, then kicks water my way. I jump back, only a few drops managing to land on my clothes. "If you don't stop, you're going to go swimming, and the ocean is cold as fuck right now."

She puts her fisted hands on her hips and lifts her chin. "You wouldn't dare."

I quirk a brow. "Try me."

She looks from me to the water, then back at me, biting her lower lip. She kicks water my way again, but not much, then dashes away toward our blankets. I laugh and chase her. Would I actually throw her in the water? Maybe one day, but not now. Things are going so well. No need to push too far or too fast.

When I catch up to her, she smiles, bends down and grabs two bottles of water from her backpack. She tosses one to me, then takes a sip from hers. Behind her, two surfers stroll down from the parking lot. She turns to watch them. While Riley enjoys surfing, it's not totally my thing, but yoga is something we used to do together.

She turns back to me and asks, "Your mom still teaching?"

I swallow the water in my mouth and place the cap back on the bottle. "Not as much, but yes. She teaches in a small studio a couple of days a week."

"That's great. I always admired how fit and flexible she is."

"Yoga'll do that for you. And more," I say. "You remember Stephens? I mean Jim. Taya's husband."

"From the barbeque? The first of you to go through the program?" She nods.

The barbeque had gone better than expected. None of my friends teased me too much about my participation in the program. Bear and Tony are a bit skeptical about me being assigned to Riley, but Jim thinks I should give it a shot and let the past be. Riley and I were still teenagers. It was her dad that really got between us. All that crap about how a kid from the trailer park would never be able to take care of his little princess. I hadn't thought Riley would have ever believed that, but it's hard to stand up to someone like her father. It's hard not to want to be treated like a princess.

I shake my head from side to side, pinching the bridge of my nose. Hasn't she already shown how much she's changed just by moving away from her parents? By living in that dumpy little studio apartment rather than take their money?

When I refocus on her, she's staring, waiting for me to continue. I scratch the back of my head and try to figure out how to explain what I want to say about Jim. "Yeah. Well, Jim had some injuries and if you haven't picked up on it, he's a very old school kinda guy. Had him try yoga. Actually, he gave it a shot right when he and Taya got together. Made a huge difference for him. Physically, mentally, emotionally. All of it. I connected him with Mom, and she told me he reaches out to her every now and then asking questions about different workouts to help with some residual issues."

"Seriously?" Riley shakes her head, a big smile on her face. "Then why is he so grumpy? You'd think he might have found some inner peace."

"Tough to say. He's gone through a lot."

A lot doesn't scratch the surface and, in retrospect, my issues are nothing compared to what Stephens has experienced. Sometimes I feel like an ass for complaining. Really, my current issues with Mason are the only thing that compares in seriousness to his. Not to mention, he's saved my ass more than once in a firefight.

Riley tosses her water bottle onto the towel and I follow suit. She places her hands above her head and stretches. The long apricot-colored T-shirt she wears barely comes up to her hips. It's practically a dress. I hope it doesn't get in her way. "Ready?"

"Yup. Warm up?"

She nods and walks a few feet away from the blanket and me so that we have space. We are parallel to one another, facing the water. Shoulder rolls are a great way to begin to loosen the body. I close my eyes and lift my shoulders toward my ears, then slowly pull my shoulder blades back and then down, taking in controlled breaths as I repeat the movement. In through the nose, out through the mouth, the briny sea air flooding my olfactory receptors.

We move on to neck stretches, continuing to focus on breathing. Standing with my legs hip-width apart, I inhale through my nose and then exhale out my mouth, slowly bending forward at the waist. My hands rest in the warm, white sand as I stretch out my lower back. This is one of the stretches I did multiple times a day when overseas, along with the standing side stretch.

Riley turns and faces me. "Which poses should we do?"

"What are you still able to do?"

"How about Downward Dog, Cobra, Warrior 1, and Navasana?"

I rub my hands together to brush the sand off of them. "Can you still do the King Pigeon?"

"Think so."

After taking a couple of centered breaths, we begin flowing through each of the poses. Plank to Cobra to Downward Dog. Soon sweat lines my forehead and I welcome the cool breeze. On occasion, I glance over at Riley to make sure she is okay. She's focused, locked in. Just like she used to be whenever we attended one of my mother's classes.

I lift my right leg high and then step it between my hands and rise up into Warrior I. I stop for a second and just watch. Riley is in Warrior I, too, sunlight reflecting off the blue sea in front of her. Strong and supple, her arms lifted high, chest open and proud. Picture perfect. She always did take my breath away. Still does.

Refocusing, I flow to the ground and then move on to Navasana, balancing on my sit bones, legs and arms extended into a V. Then I move forward into King Pigeon. Riley struggles a bit with the hip-opening pose but doesn't give up. When we are done, we both grab our bottles of water. Sweat drips down our necks.

"That was awesome. I haven't done this in so long, and on the beach no less. There's something serene about being out here." Riley folds her arms and shifts from foot to foot. "I want to see if I can still do Scorpion pose."

I raise an eyebrow. "Ambitious if you haven't done it in a while." I remember the first time she nailed that pose in class. The strength it takes to balance on your forearms while inverting yourself and doing a backbend makes it a pretty big accomplishment. She hadn't been able to help herself back then. She'd let out a big whoop before collapsing to the ground. The whole class had cracked up and then given her a standing ovation.

"Go big or go home, right? It's kind of the Texas way." She grins. "I've got this."

I shrug. "Just don't hurt yourself."

"I know my limits." Riley gets down on her knees and refocuses. She begins to get in position, balancing on her forearms, and she kicks her legs up in the air. When she starts to bend at the knees, bringing her feet toward her head, I see her wobble. As she arches to try to balance, I place my hand on her abdomen to steady her and between gravity and her movement, that dress-like shirt starts to lift.

"What the fuck, Lucas?" Riley falls sideways and springs to her feet. "What the hell are you doing?"

"I was just trying to help you." I stiffen, immediately replaying what just happened in my mind. Did I touch her in some sexual way without her permission? No, my hands weren't anywhere near her breasts. Nor was any part of my body pressing against hers.

"I told you I wasn't ready for that . . . that kind of touching." Her arms go around her stomach like she's protecting something precious.

I hold up both hands, palms facing her with splayed fingers. "I only wanted to keep you from falling over. Swear it."

Her chin wobbles like she might cry. "Well, it sure felt like that kind of touching." She throws on her sweatshirt, then bends over to collect her things. "I'd like to go home now."

I watch her march away from me back to the truck. Every damn thing I do is wrong. No matter how hard I try, it's like I'll never get it right.

My throat tightens.

Or be good enough. Her father's words replay in my head. *Just a stupid kid from the trailer park who will never amount to anything.*

Grabbing the towel, I shove it into the bag and collect my crap. Each breath I take is sharp, shallow. So much for a fresh start. Damn woman walked away from me again. Just like last time. Who knows what will set her off because I sure as shit have no idea. And then what? She'll walk right out the door breaking my heart. Mason's heart.

This is exactly what Lisa had a problem with. Granted, maybe I overshared with my ex-wife, even possibly exaggerated about Riley's cruelty. But still, Lisa is Mason's mother and like me, she only wants the best for her son. Maybe I should listen to her instincts since mine clearly suck.

I lean back and fall onto the sand, resting my face in my hands. Lisa. The first sign that something was wrong in our marriage was when she pulled away from me physically, didn't want me to touch her. Is this the first sign our relationship will never work? Riley doesn't want me to touch her, just like Lisa didn't want me to touch her. They're so different, those two. Dark and light. Different personalities. Different hopes and dreams. There's really only one common denominator—me.

Maybe Riley's dad was right. I'm the problem. Two women walking away, there's really no other explanation.

CHAPTER TEN

Riley

AFTER WE'D GOTTEN back from the beach, I'd showered and retreated to my room. I spent the rest of the day applying for jobs online and reading, then tossing from one side of the bed to the other during the night. Now I'm hiding under the covers, continuing to avoid my husband.

Why did he have to ruin everything? We'd been fine, having a nice time, doing our yoga. Why'd he have to put his big paws on me? And why did the ways he helped always have to be way more than I wanted?

I punch the pillow and scream into it. It's not his fault. Well, not completely. I'm partly to blame. But I'm just not ready to explain my whole medical history. Which means I need to be more understanding when things become uncomfortable.

My head jerks up when the *thunk* of three knocks on my bedroom door fill the air. "We need to leave soon," Lucas says.

"Why? What for?"

"We have the counseling session to go to in a bit."

My fingers clench the cotton material of the pillow as my eyes widen. "Counseling?"

"Yeah, the mandated marriage counseling that's part of the program." I can hear him kick at the carpet through the door.

I should really have read that contract more thoroughly. I remember counseling being mentioned, but not that it was mandatory. I get out of bed and open my bedroom door a crack. "For some reason, I thought that was optional."

Lucas snorts and stomps down the stairs. "Wishful thinking. Be ready to go in fifteen."

He doesn't wait for my answer.

I get dressed, picking out a skirt with a poppy design on it and a silk tank top. I pull my hair into a ponytail and am marching down the stairs twelve minutes later. I'm not even to the bottom of the stairs before he's heading out the door to the truck. He hits the remote to unlock the doors and I grab the handle, pull my door open, and hop inside.

Lucas gets behind the wheel and we ride to the therapist's office. The silence crackles between us, tension coming off Lucas in waves. Of course he's angry. But he was the one who grabbed at me without permission, not the other way around. Yet if I'd told him, he might've completely avoided touching me altogether. Not the way I wanted to feel either.

He turns on the radio and Shania Twain starts singing about being a woman. I reach over and snap it off and look out my window. Definitely not the song I need to hear right now. It doesn't matter how much I feel like a woman, my body has betrayed me too many times to trust it.

When we get to the building, Lucas gets out of the truck and walks to the building without even looking behind him to see if I'm following. We step into the office with such sharp precision it's clear to any observer there are problems. The therapist's fake smile doesn't help matters either. Yet I offer my own. Lucas takes a seat on the leather couch, taking up half of it with his long legs and broad shoulders. I scoot into the corner at the opposite end, as far from him as I can get.

"Welcome, Mr. and Mrs. Craiger. I'm Dr. Stehman." The therapist takes a seat on the chair across from the couch. She's an angular woman, tall and thin, with short blond hair and tortoiseshell glasses. She has on a straight skirt that hits her mid-calf and a light summer sweater. Her office is like her. Calm and professional. Classic in style. "Congratulations on your arrangement."

"Thanks," Lucas mutters, complete with a dash of sarcasm.

Dr. Stehman quirks a brow. "Looks like I might have my work cut out for me today."

She absolutely does. I hate therapy. I hate talking about my feelings. I hate the sad looks of concern on the therapists' faces. It doesn't change anything. No amount of talking is going to make my GI tract behave like everyone else's. No amount of sharing is going to give me back the life I thought I was going to have. Been there. Done that. It doesn't change a damn thing. So, I pick at a cuticle as the therapist goes through some of the specifics of each session as they relate to the Issued Partner Program.

"Lucas, why did you join the program?"

"Ma'am, that's in the application." He clears his throat. "I saw my two friends find success with it, so figured I'd give it a go."

The therapist leans back in her chair. "Why?"

"Why what?" He looks over to me as if I have some kind of answer for him. I shrug and turn away. I know my reasons. He has to come up with his own.

"Did you not have success dating?" The therapist offers a polite smile, prompting him.

He rubs his hands on his pants. He's nervous. "Got divorced, tired of the groupies, wanted someone who could handle the life and be a good match for me. And for Mason, my son."

Groupies?

My jaw clenches and my pulse starts to race. Not sure why I thought Lucas had remained celibate since his divorce. Well, maybe I just didn't want to think of him sleeping with other people. But groupies?

"And what about you, Riley?" Stehman turns to angle her body toward me.

I stare at her, blinking excessively. Right. Of course I'm going to have to speak. I can't exactly tell the truth. I can't tell them I needed health insurance and this seemed like the best way to get it fast. Not just because I'm concerned what would happen if the program committee found out, but I also don't want to hurt Lucas. I turn toward my husband and find him staring at me, his brow furrowed. What would he think if I told him? The blood leaves my face and my stomach cramps. Come on, Riley. Figure something out to say. "Dating sucks. People are cruel. I figured the program would assign me to someone who actually wanted a relationship versus a casual hookup."

Lucas looks away, some of the stiffness leaving his shoulders.

"And how are things going for you two? There was definitely some tension when you arrived." Dr. Stehman leans back in her chair and looks from Lucas to me. Nice understatement.

"We had an argument yesterday," Lucas says.

"What about?" Stehman asks.

"Just Lucas thinking he needs to fix stuff." The words came out before I could stop them.

Dr. Stehman places her hands down on her thighs. "Does Lucas wanting to help bother you?"

"Does it bother you when someone automatically thinks you're incapable of handling your life on your own?" Truth is, my response was fear based because I am actually afraid of him rejecting me.

"Whoa. I never said that." Lucas raises his hands in the air. "You were about to fall and I caught you."

I close my eyes and rub my temples. "Did I ask you to? Did I give you permission to touch me? We agreed . . ."

Lucas slouches into his corner of the couch. "You are going to give me whiplash, Riley. One second you're holding hands with me and resting your head on my shoulder. The next second I try to keep you from toppling over and you lose it. What the hell is going on?"

Dr. Stehman turns to me. "Riley, is that true? Are you sending Lucas mixed signals?"

"No. I said I wasn't ready for that kind of touching and I'm not." Being next to Lucas stirs something in me, something I was afraid had died in these last few years. But I can't bear the thought of the look on his face when he sees those scars or the way his hand will freeze when he feels them.

Lucas is shaking his head. "There's more going on here. There's something you're not telling me. Some things just don't add up."

A cold sweat starts to break out on my forehead. "Like what?"

"What were you doing in that tiny studio apartment? That's not the kind of place you're used to. I can't imagine your parents not getting you a decent place to live."

Oh, they wanted to give me a decent place to live, all right. Unfortunately it was with them, under their constantly watchful eyes. "I wanted a fresh start. And I wanted to do it on my own."

"Fresh from what?" Lucas asks.

"What about you?" I counter. "You're not telling the whole story here either. You were looking for someone to help you with your custody issues. A wife would certainly help your case."

Lucas rears back and Dr. Stehman lets out a little gasp.

If only I could stuff the words back in my mouth the second they hit the air.

CHAPTER ELEVEN

Lucas

WHAT. THE. ACTUAL. Fuck.

Air rushes out of my lungs as if I'd been kicked by a horse. My fingers dig into the armrest of the couch. Riley thinks I married her to help out with Mason? Guess she forgot the reason I'm going to court. It's because she's in my life, not despite it. "Marrying you is the reason Lisa wants a legal custody agreement."

Where is this coming from? What happened to the woman who wanted to go with me to see the lawyer? Who said we'd show Lisa we could be a family for Mason? I rub both hands over my face. "Look. We're supposed to be working things out here. Not making them worse."

"Mr. and Mrs. Craiger, there are obviously some underlying issues here." The therapist flips through the file, reads something, then closes the folder. "I do notice you both knew each other as teenagers. But let me be forthright, even the smallest lies will cost you both. The committee doesn't take people joining the program for personal gain lightly. If you did in fact sign up to help with your custody case, Lucas, you could be dishonorably discharged."

My body tenses and it's as if all the oxygen in the room dissipates. Be kicked out of the military? Fuck, no. Not after everything I've gone through to get where I am.

Losing my job would mean losing my son.

And my purpose.

I level the therapist with a look. "I assure you that is not why I joined. I'm sure the committee will find legal paperwork that is dated to corroborate my statement."

Could this day get any worse? Talk therapy is supposed to help but it's making everything worse. I guess it only helps when everyone is being honest, which Riley definitely isn't. There's something about her stomach, the way she constantly leans forward, arms clasped around her middle, like right now. And the way she panics if my hands come anywhere near it. Somehow it's tied up with her moving out here and that stupid apartment. She's always been one to deflect, but I never would have thought she'd deflect in a way that would hurt Mason. I thought she really liked him and I could tell he liked her.

My gaze runs over my wife. She's pale again, and there's a sheen of sweat on her forehead. Something is wrong. She's in pain. I reach out a hand and place it on her shoulder. "You okay?"

"Peachy," she snaps. "I don't want or need your concern or any special treatment."

My mouth drops open. Uh, what do I say to that? How is asking if someone is okay the wrong thing to do? I raise my eyebrows at Dr. Stehman who also watches Riley, hoping she might have a suggestion.

Instead, her noncommittal smile and concerned facial expressions fade. She's cool. Assessing. Riley seems to notice, too, and fidgets. My wife's shoulders slump and she lets out an audible sigh. "Actually, I'm not peachy. I'm not feeling so great. Could we reschedule?"

"Of course," Dr. Stehman says.

My heel bounces against the floor as we set a new date, my gaze shifting between my wife and the floor. Don't want to upset her, but I'm worried. Once we are all set, Riley and I exit the office. I stay behind her, shoving my hands into my pockets because I'm not sure what else to do. And at least if they are restricted by the denim material, I might not overstep and make her feel incapable.

The ride home is as silent and tense as the one to the therapist's office. I steal glances over at Riley. Her skin is even paler and she's hunched over even more, arms still crossed over her stomach. What can I do to make her feel better?

I stare out the windshield and my mind drifts back to our appointment and that pause before she answered why she joined the program. Is that where the problem lies? Her answer was fine, once she said it. So why did it seem so difficult for her to admit to? Especially since it's in line with my reasons. It's not the first time the question has come up. She had to have said something on the application about why she applied. Unless, of course, she's lying and had to scramble to remember what she'd said before. A cold knot forms in the pit of my stomach.

When we get back to the house, her door opens and she's getting out practically before I can put the truck in park.

She's upstairs by the time I get in the house. The door of the upstairs bathroom slams shut. Dread owns me, pushing against me like an invisible gale, attempting to reverse my steps back to the garage and into my truck. My stomach is locked up tight, nothing getting in or out, and I'm sweating through the button-down shirt.

But unless I can turn back time and drag the sun from the sky, the chips have to fall where they may. I just hope if given enough space, Riley will open up to me before the stress of watching her suffer eats me alive.

CHAPTER TWELVE

Riley

AT FIRST I was shocked to receive a text from Marge inviting me out for coffee with Inara and Taya. I'd only met them once at the barbeque. They'd been nice enough considering the way Lucas had sprung our marriage on all of them and the fact that they seemed to be well aware of our history. I'm sure his version of the events didn't exactly portray me in a good light, so I'm relieved they accept me as part of the group. I want so much to explain my version to them and to Lucas, but I've seen too often how people react to finding out I have a chronic illness. It goes one of two ways. They walk out because it's too much to handle or they get cloying and try to wrap me up in cotton wool like I might break apart at any moment.

My plan for the day had been to remain in bed, especially with the flare-up that started in the therapist's office kicking in, even if my new bedroom is so much like my old bedroom at my parents' place I feel like I might suffocate. Fatigue is a common symptom of Crohn's disease and it is kicking my butt at the moment. I want to rest, take a beat, and maybe keep this flare-up from getting any worse than it has to be.

On the other hand, stress and anxiety can make a flare-up worse and the atmosphere around the house is definitely stressful. I still can't believe what I said at therapy. Never did it cross my mind that Lucas married me to help out his case. And he's right. There wouldn't be a custody case if it wasn't for me. But will telling him the truth—the whole truth—help or hurt that case? If Lisa is already having concerns about Mason having a new stepparent, how much worse will it be once she discovers I also have a chronic disease?

And now they might use what I just said to kick Lucas out of the military? A dishonorable discharge? I didn't miss his reaction when Dr. Stehman said that. He looked stunned. Frozen. Then he went so cold and calm, and it felt like the temperature in the room dropped ten degrees. He's barely spoken since coming back from counseling and even went as far as disinviting me from going to the lawyer's with him because he wanted to handle everything himself.

Which I should probably understand, since it's how I feel too. I want to handle my own life. Talk to him on my own terms, not be forced. Especially considering the way I'm feeling right now. The last thing I want is him hovering around me, babying me as I ride out a bad spell. So I've been keeping to my teenage dream bedroom when he's in the house, creeping out when I hear him leave. It's not like he's so much as knocked on my door either. The few times I've walked into a room when he's there, he's walked out.

So, yeah. Maybe some time away from Lucas would be a good thing. Although, a café wouldn't have been my choice. Or my second or third. Why did every social event seem to center around food?

But the place they wanted to meet, Marigold's, is charming. It's a great mix of rustic and modern with wide-planked wooden floors, exposed brick walls, and mid-century modern chrome-and-leather booths and stools. And the aroma! The air is delicious with the scent of coffee and cookies and cakes.

I take a second to breathe it all in, checking to see that my sundress covered with orange hibiscus flowers is in order.

"Riley."

I look toward the back-left corner and spot Marge waving. I return the gesture and head toward her, taking a quick second to glance at the menu on the wall behind the counter. Thank the Lord, they have toast. I'll be fine.

"Hey," Taya stands and gives me a hug, all dark hair and snapping eyes. Next to her is a sleeping baby in a stroller.

I blink rapidly. That is one big-ass baby and while Taya isn't petite, I really can't imagine how she gave birth to a child that size, or how anyone could give birth to a baby that size.

The group erupts into laughter and I'm curious as to what I missed. So, I pull out a chair and take a seat, my gaze bouncing between the three women. Inara places her hand on my forearm. "We all have the same reaction whenever we look at Otto. Just looking at him makes me want to cross my legs."

"Was I that obvious?" I let out a low groan. How freakin' embarrassing.

Taya chuckles. "No worries, as long as those reactions are hidden from Jim. I swear my husband acts as if having a kid that's off the growth charts is some kind of paternal badge of honor. Like he was the only one involved in making this kid."

Jim jokes around? He has a sense of humor? The last time I met him, he was so impassive, I figured he was the group member with no personality. Definitely the complete opposite of Inara's husband. Tony has enough personality for the whole team, although from what I heard at the barbeque, Lucas has quite the personality too.

If only I could see that side of him more. When we were in high school, he'd been fun. I remember laughing so hard at something he said, I was worried I'd wet my pants. Some of the stories I'd heard made it sound like he and Martinez were the lives of the party wherever they were. I was having a hard time reconciling that with the taciturn man whose back was so tense I could see the muscles bunch up under his shirt when we were together.

"Did you want to order anything? It's on me." Marge waves the server over.

"Uh, just water. And maybe some toast."

As subtle as Marge tries to be, I catch the quick glance she shoots at Taya. They definitely have noticed what I eat or don't eat and have talked about it. Damn it. Should have stayed home. That way, no one would have questions.

Another reminder why I like to keep myself to myself, thank you very much. I have no desire to be the topic of anyone's conversation.

Inara's phone pings, and she picks it up and then taps furiously at it. "Carajo. I don't understand this fool. Can someone please explain to me why I agreed to marry my husband? Was I drugged? Hypnotized?"

"What'd he do now?" Taya asks, grinning.

"Mira." Inara turns the screen to face the rest of us. "The idiot knocked down our bathroom. Decided to remodel it. Without talking to me first."

We all peer at the photo of a bathroom, or what's left of one. The door is off its hinges and leaning against the wall in the hallway. There's an empty hole where the sink should be. Same with the toilet. And half the walls are missing tiles.

My eyebrows lift and I look at Taya and Marge, who seem to be hiding smiles behind strategically held cups of coffee. I wouldn't want to be Tony if he doesn't get that bathroom put back together. Inara sure as hell appears to be a woman who might storm out of here to open a can of whoop ass on her husband if he doesn't. Boy, do I like her. Maybe she could knock some sense into my spouse.

Then again, when she gets his side of the story, she might turn on me too.

Inara turns to me. "Just a heads-up, I'm sure he'll con Lucas into helping him. Don't be afraid to tell Tony the answer is no. And don't leave it up to your husband to say so. Those two are like children. They can't be left to make their own decisions. I swear Mason is the most mature out of the three of them."

A soft laugh escapes my lips. "I don't know any of them that well, but it actually sounds like it would be fun to watch."

Inara waves a careless hand in the air. "Yeah, when it's someone else's husband. But when it's your own . . . you'll be in the same boat as me, wondering where your common sense went."

"How are things going with Lucas?" Marge asks.

I slouch a bit and fiddle with the napkin in front of me. "They're going."

"Can't be as bad as Jim and I were at first. We fought so much when we first moved in together. Two total strangers trying to make heads or tails of a crazy situation." Taya takes a sip of her coffee, then puts it down. "Though, you two dated in the past, right?"

Hoo boy. Here we go. If only I knew what they already know, what Lucas has told them or any of the men. "When we were kids."

I'm grateful for the temporary distraction of the server bringing over our food, but even after I take a bite of my toast, the women are all staring at me. Guess they want more info. I search my brain for the most bare-bones version of our history. "We dated in high school. Broke up during senior year."

"Kind of like Bear and me. We dated in high school. I got pregnant, thanks to having too much fun at the senior prom. We split up after our oldest daughter was born but made our way back to one another." Marge smiles and her whole face lights up from the inside. "Sometimes you never know where the future will bring you."

"That man was lost without you. Still would be. He worships the ground you walk on." Inara shakes her head. "And he happens to be more mature than the dingbat I got stuck with."

Marge elbows her. "And you love him."

Inara grins ear to ear. A similar light to the one that shines on Marge's face is shining on hers. "I do."

It would be nice to feel like that, to have the thought of someone light up my face, to have someone who can drive me up the wall only for me to laugh about it with friends. But the fact is, that will never happen for me. I know that now. It's not like I haven't tried. Truthfully, who would want to spend their life with a person who will get sick off and on for the rest of their life? I wouldn't want to burden anyone with my illness and the struggles it causes. I can barely deal with it on my own most days. And the kind of person who would want that is probably the kind of person who would want to wrap me up in Bubble Wrap and put me on a shelf. Like my parents.

I pick at the piece of toast, popping a section of the crust into my mouth.

Taya must have seen some of what I'm feeling on my face. "Riley, you can talk to us. This life isn't easy. Forget the program. Wait until the guys get deployed or go on training missions." Taya takes a bite of her Danish and continues once she swallows. "It can be the loneliest feeling in the world."

"Not to mention raising the children by yourself." Marge *thunks* her coffee mug down with a bit too much force, sloshing a bit onto the table. "You'll learn to unstop toilets and how to mow the lawn and to fix the damn mower when it breaks, among other things you'd never thought you'd be doing."

"And that's just the day-to-day stuff. Because there's also the danger. Jim's been hurt, had a severe TBI. I think they've all been shot at least once." Taya stops and takes a deep breath, then looks down at her son. "They even had a former teammate who was killed."

I suck in a sharp breath, my chest tightening. The same way it had at the beach when I came across the surfing program for the Gold Star families. Lucas could die. He could walk out the door one day and never walk back through it again. The thought claws away at my insides, and my stomach lurches. Part of it's the Crohn's, but the other part is thinking about what losing Lucas would mean. I set the crust of toast I was about to eat down.

Someone places her hand on top of mine. "We have each other, okay? Anything you feel, any worries, anything you need help with, just ask."

I follow the hand up to find Inara looking at me. I nod, fighting back the tears forming. These women are kind. And strong. And they rely on one another. Not one of them is weak. How could they be? They're taking care of their families, supporting their husbands, all while knowing they might never see them again. Do I have that type of strength in me?

Marge slaps the table. "Enough of that. Now, Riley, curious. What's with the toast? Are you and Lucas having a bit too much fun?"

It takes me a moment to figure out what she means. The water I had been drinking goes down the wrong way and I choke. Marge quirks a brow. Holy shit. While I expected maybe a comment about what I was eating, this wasn't the direction I'd anticipated. "Just an upset stomach," I say, one of my usual dodges.

"Of the nine-month variety?" Inara sits back, narrowing her eyes as if analyzing my reaction.

They think I might be pregnant. I can feel the heat climbing up my cheeks, thinking about what we would need to do to get me that way. "Uh, no. We haven't . . . done that yet."

Liquid sputters and I turn my head to find Taya wiping coffee from her chin. "You two haven't had sex yet?"

Marge slaps her on the shoulder. "Look who's talking. You and Jim certainly took your time."

Taya starts to protest, but I brush at some of the crumbs my toast has left on the table. "No, we haven't. Everything's still awkward. And his ex-wife is pushing for some sort of custody arrangement that Lucas is super unhappy about. Actually, he's at the lawyer's now. Figuring out what his options are." I bite the corner of my lower lip. Maybe I should've kept that to myself.

"That makes sense. No wonder he's been moody." Inara drums her purple-painted nails against the table. "Tony said he's been closed off, touchy even. I think those two even had some sort of fight at work the other day and they're like brothers."

I'm sure I'm part of the reason and my stomach twists again. No point in adding that to the conversation.

"Must be tough becoming a stepmom," Taya says. "Hell, it's tough being a new mom. Wait and see."

That is not something I'm focused on. I adore Mason and love being a stepmom to him, but as far as other children go? Well, I won't be having any. Not after all the medical procedures I've had. It's too risky. With the resections I've had, the pressure of carrying a child could cause more harm to my intestines. Not to mention the medications that help control my Crohn's can harm a baby. No. I've gone through enough. I still go through enough. Having a ready-made family is perfect for me. Mason is perfect for me. He's a great kid. God, I hope the lawyer has some way to help Lucas in all this.

I force out a breath, my shoulders sagging. I can only imagine what the thought of losing him must be doing to Lucas. I promised Lucas we'd make this marriage work for the mandated year, make the court see Lucas was a good father. I intend to keep that promise.

I slump back in my seat, realizing keeping that promise

means apologizing for shoving him away at the beach and for what I said in therapy. If the shirt shifted any more, his hand would've hit the scars. The fact that they're ugly is bad enough. Having to explain them before I'm ready would be even worse. So instead, I went with that old idea that a good offense is better than a defense and pitched a fit and continued that fit right on through to the counseling appointment. Lucas isn't the one who's putting his pride before what's best for a terrific little boy who deserves to have his mom and his dad in his life. That would be me.

I swallow past the lump in my throat, hoping my husband will forgive me, and return to the conversation, which has luckily moved on to exactly what Tony is doing to Inara's bathroom.

CHAPTER THIRTEEN

Riley

THE HOUSE IS empty when I arrive home, a note on the fridge informing me Lucas had a meeting. Which meant I had time to decide my next move. And that is to make things right. I don't want to be the reason Lucas loses custody of Mason. But sitting here on the couch, staring out the window, waiting to spot his truck, is doing little for my anxiety.

I need a distraction. I reach out and grab my laptop from the coffee table. Might as well use my time productively. Opening my email, I pull up the messages from the two companies who'd offered me jobs.

Clicking on a new document, I begin to type out all the information into two columns. Pay. Retirement benefits. Insurance options. Paid training. Days off. And the list goes on. Then I start adding technical requirements.

By the time I'm done, Lucas pulls into the driveway and I steel myself for what comes next. The front door clicks open as I close my laptop and place it back on the coffee table. My husband walks inside, his head turns in my direction, and after a brief pause, he keeps walking.

"Lucas, can we talk?" I ask, keeping my voice level and even, although my heart is hammering.

He stops, the muscles in his back tensing. He's so strong. He always was. Strong and steady and sensible. It's why I broke up with him. I knew how he'd behave when he found out how ill I was. What he'd sacrifice to stay by my side. I couldn't have it. It wouldn't have been fair.

He turns to me, face impassive except for a pronounced tic of his jaw. "Tried that. Didn't go so well for me. Might lose my kid and my job because of talking."

I look down at my hands. "I know. I'm sorry. I . . . I regret what I said. I'll call Dr. Stehman and tell her I was just angry and looking for a way to lash out."

He just lingers there, hands jammed into the pockets of his jeans, leaning against the wall with one shoulder, watching me with those chocolate-brown eyes. Since he continues to remain silent, I push on. "How did things go with the lawyer?"

"It went."

"Is there anything I can do to help? I want to be there for you and for Mason. Please let me know the best way to do that. I would love to be there with you when you meet with the lawyer next time if you think that would make things easier."

He shakes his head. "I . . . I didn't know you *wanted* to go. I didn't know if you wanted to have anything to do with me."

I get up and walk over to where he stands, then reach up and place my hand on his jaw. I turn it so he faces me, looks at me, sees me. "Mason is the best and you're a great dad. There's no reason we can't provide a loving second home for him."

He takes my hand. "I hope Lisa sees it that way."

I give that hand a squeeze. "We'll make her see it."

For a moment we stand there, hands locked together, close enough that I can feel the heat from his body, smell the woodsy scent of his cologne. I place my other hand on his chest and feel the thump of his heart, strong and steady against my palm. And those muscles! The man is made out of marble. "I, uh, want to apologize for what happened on the beach the other day."

His muscles stiffen under my hand. He's still angry. I understand why a bit more now that I've had time to think about it. I didn't trust him. I'm still not sure I do, but if I want him to trust me, I'm going to have to try. It's a two-way street.

I want him to see me. Really see me. All of me. That means he'll have questions. Questions I think I'm ready to answer now. I suck in a deep breath and pop the top button of his shirt. The thump of his heart picks up pace.

"Riley?" His voice comes out gravelly and deep.

I pop the next button. And the next.

His breath comes in short bursts, his hands clenched at his sides. I slide the shirt off his arms and stare at the chiseled body before me. So masculine. So powerful. So different from when we were kids and yet still so familiar.

My sex pulsates, my nipples harden the longer I look. But anxiety is there too. I've had a man want me before only to run out when he saw me naked. I swallow past the fear. That man wasn't Lucas. Lucas won't do that.

At least I hope he won't.

I reach down to take his hand again and my eyes catch sight of the bulge between his legs. The corners of my mouth curl up. Some things don't change. I know exactly what's behind the material of his pants. My breath quickens at the thought of feeling him inside me again. He'd been my first and the few other encounters I'd had never quite measured up.

Taking Lucas by the wrist, I lead him up the stairs and into my bedroom. He doesn't say a word. Just follows.

Once inside, I push him down gently to take a seat on the edge of the bed. My body hums with both a sexual and nervous energy. Here we go. Moment of truth.

I reach behind and pull down on the zipper to my dress, watching as the orange-flowered garment falls to the floor. I inhale deeply and stand straight in nothing but a lace thong, completely exposed to the air, to the world, to Lucas.

The room remains quiet, every creak of the house sounding louder than the blare of a train's horn. I bite my lip and look to Lucas. His fingers grasp the blanket covering my bed, brows furrowed as he concentrates on my abdomen, at the scars that crisscross there.

Christ.

This was a mistake.

But before I can react to the awkwardness of the situation, Lucas leans forward and wraps a big, muscled arm around my waist and pulls me forward. He nuzzles into me and gently kisses the scarred flesh. "Is this why you got so mad at me on the beach? And shut me down on the Ferris wheel? These scars?"

I try to say yes, but the word won't come out. Instead, my throat tightens and tears congregate at the corners of my eyes. I look toward the ceiling to keep them from spilling out. But it's no use.

"Riley?"

I swallow hard and hold my eyelids open, praying the air will dry out the tears. Lucas kisses my stomach once again and I slowly move my head until I'm looking down at him. My hands rest on his shoulders and he pulls me down so I am sitting on top of him.

He tilts my chin with a finger so my eyes meet his. "I'm sorry for whatever caused this, but know it doesn't change how I see you in any way, shape, or form. I love you. I always have."

"I . . . um—"

He places a finger against my lips. "You don't have to explain tonight. From the time you jumped on that wild mare to when you'd backtalk your father whenever he had something to say about the trailer park I grew up in, you've shown yourself to be one of the strongest and most fearless people I know."

Echoing the words from the love letter that is still in my wallet breaks the hold fear has on me. This man just recited what he wrote me fifteen years ago as if he'd come up with the words this second. Nothing could touch me deeper, reach my soul on the level he has. I offer him a soft smile. "I'm really glad we're getting a second chance."

"Me too."

He leans forward to kiss me, but I pull back. "Not yet."

My body aches with need, but if there's one thing I remember after all these years, it's how much fun teasing Lucas can be. It's been years since I felt sexy and confident enough to play those kinds of games with a man. The touch of Lucas's lips against my stomach makes me feel brave. I want to be in control, to show him how strong I still can be.

I push him hard back onto the bed. He scoots back and I reposition so I'm once again straddling his hips, my pussy resting on the bulge of his thick cock in his pants.

"Riley—"

I cut him off with a kiss and when his hands cup my neck, I pull away. Grabbing his hands, I place them above his head. "No touching."

"Not fair."

"Shh." I bring my finger up to his lips and kiss him again, moving to his jawline, and neck as I grind against him.

"Riley." The deep tone and desperation of his voice causes the hum of need in my body to become stronger.

I nip at his earlobe and he bucks, his fingers grabbing onto my blanket as if he's holding on for dear life. Sitting up,

I reposition myself so I'm sitting on his thighs. His pupils are large, his chest heaving with every breath.

Slowly I unbutton and unzip his dress pants, earning me a nice hiss from my husband. Lucas drops his head back and tugs on the blanket as I remove his clothes, revealing his huge erection, pained and full. Inside, all I can feel is a pulsing need, an arousal so strong I can barely function.

I lean over him, my body gently grazing his hardness and he growls. When my lips are pressed against his earlobe, I nip him once more. "Your turn."

He instantly flips me over and buries his head into my neck, hands roving over my skin. He makes his way down my body and rips off my underwear, then buries his face between my legs.

"Holy, fucking shit."

Yeah, not exactly the sexiest words to ever leave my mouth, but it has been over five years since a man has touched me, much less devoured me.

My back arches as his tongue flattens against me, rubbing my clit. My body tenses, the need too strong. My fingers tug at his hair, my nails dig into his scalp. "Don't stop."

Lucas is ravenous. I grab my breasts and pinch my nipples. A deep growl catches my attention and I look down to find Lucas staring up at me. He sucks my clit into his mouth while his tongue swipes back and forth. Then I feel him push his finger inside of me, and that's all it takes. I climax instantly as my back bows off the mattress, and I scream out his name. "Lucas!"

My thighs clench at the sides of his head, but he doesn't stop. Not until my body is spent. Lucas's breathing turns uneven and rapid. Grabbing his cock, he roughly strokes it up and down, sliding his thumb over the tip and smearing precum all over as he stares at me spread out deliciously before him.

Then he stops and looks around as if coming out of a trance. He scratches his head and when his gaze lands on his pants, he grabs them and pulls out his wallet. When he tosses it back to the ground, I notice the foil package in his hand.

Oh. A condom.

I bite my lower lip and moan as I watch him tear open the package and slide on the latex. Crawling back up, he wraps me up in his arms while lowering his mouth to mine. His fingers sink into my hair and he kisses me hard, dominating me.

Feeling more than a little desperate, I fight back against his questing tongue and lips. Breaking the kiss, he slides his hand down between my legs, spreading my wet lips, then nudges his cock against my entrance, slowly pushing inside.

I lock my legs around his waist and thrust my hips up, sliding him even deeper. Lucas captures both of my wrists in one hand and pins them above my head as he thrusts fast and hard. Then he takes my mouth in the most tender and gentle kiss I have ever experienced, sliding his tongue against mine.

"God, you're so tight, Riley, so fucking perfect." He

grunts, picking up speed until he's slamming into me at full force.

He explodes not long after, mumbling how I was squeezing his orgasm from him and loving the feel of my pussy on his cock. He smiles a lopsided grin followed by a laugh that spoke for him. He's wrecked and satisfied, and he couldn't look more vulnerable if he opened up his chest, pulled out his heart and handed it to me.

Yes, I'm definitely glad for this second chance.

CHAPTER FOURTEEN

Lucas

RUSSO'S IS PACKED tonight. Even the servers are rushing around more than usual. Although to be honest, the last time I was here was three years ago. Maybe this is a typical Thursday night. Russo's is not the kind of place I go to all the time. It's a 'special occasion' kind of restaurant, which is why we're here. Riley deserved to be taken somewhere elegant, somewhere special, somewhere I couldn't go in a T-shirt and jeans, somewhere her father wouldn't think I'd ever be able to afford or appreciate.

To say her apology rocked my world would be a world-class understatement and I'm not just talking about the sex, although that was mind-blowing. Those scars. She's been through something. Something hard. Something it's not easy for her to talk about. She's trusting me now and letting me know I can trust her with Mason.

Her support touched me in a way I don't expect. Something warm unfurled in my chest and the tightness went away. Could we make a home for Mason? A family for all three of us? Is Riley really here for the long haul? Maybe I should stop looking for signs that she's going to leave. It's possible that I've been too sensitive. Lisa's engagement did bother me. Not that I expected my ex-wife to remain single the rest of her life, but there was a sting to it when I found out she was getting remarried. One more sign that I wasn't good enough, that I'd failed as a man. I'd had the same feeling with Riley when she walked away from me at the beach, but she's still here and she's telling me she wants to be there for me and for my son.

I look to my right as Riley fidgets, adjusting the strap of her dress. The silky apricot fabric shines against her honeyed skin. "You look stunning."

She dips her chin and smiles. Since when has she ever been shy? Or maybe I don't compliment her enough. Gotta address that. She deserves to know how beautiful she is. All the time.

"Right this way." The maître d' leads us through the maze of tables to our seats.

The place is beautiful. White tablecloths starched within an inch of their lives and flickering candles. Glinting silver and carpet so soft I feel like I'm sinking into it. It's pricey, too, but I have a lot to make up for. Stomping around like a damn fool instead of trying to make this marriage work. Luckily, Taya was able to pull some strings and get us in here. The manager used to work over at Shaken and Stirred, the restaurant she works at.

Riley peruses the menu and lowers it after a minute, her eyebrows raised. "Um, Lucas. You know we could've gone out for burgers, right?"

"Price isn't an issue. Get whatever you want." If only her father could be here. Certainly a far cry from the poor kid who wasn't good enough for his daughter he thought I'd always be.

I sit back in my chair and relax for the first time in days. The soft ambient music and warm dim lighting help. The waiter approaches, his black uniform neatly ironed and crisp. Funny the things I notice thanks to the military.

"May I take your order?" He looks expectantly at Riley.

Riley glances at the menu once more, then hands it to the waiter. "I'll take the salmon, but can I substitute white rice for the potatoes?"

"Yes, ma'am." He turns to face me. "And for you, sir?"

"The butter chicken and pilau rice. Also, can I get two glasses of Moselle?" Another thing I wouldn't mind Riley's father seeing. I know what kind of wine to order with fish and chicken. Not exactly something he'd expect from a kid who'd grown up poor, like me.

Riley holds up her hand. "Just one glass. I'm going to stick with water."

Damn it. I probably should have asked her what kind of wine she wanted instead of deciding for her. The Moselle is pretty midrange for Russo's wine list. After the waiter leaves, I lean closer to Riley. "Don't worry about the cost. Please, if you want a different wine, we can order it."

"Lucas, I'm okay. I'd just prefer water." She smiles and reaches out to put her hand over mine.

I hold still, relishing her touch even if it's only this small gesture. She looks like she's lost some weight. I know she's been under the weather, but don't really know what's been wrong. Maybe it has something to do with those scars, the ones she showed me, but hasn't been willing to talk about yet. Not that there's been an opportunity really. Work has had me so busy. I hope that's not what's making her feel ill, that it's not causing her too much stress. Some people aren't cut out for dealing with the crazy and inconsistent schedules Special Forces members have. Hell, most people aren't. There's a reason the divorce rate is so high. That's part of the reason the program exists in the first place.

I rub my thumb gently over the back of her hand, my eyes locking with Riley's, and I get lost for a second in their endless blue. She is beautiful, but there's a sadness there. A smile that never reaches those amazing eyes. I've noticed it before. Whatever happened in the years we were apart, whatever made those scars, it's past time to see what needs to be done to fix it. "I know the whole program can be daunting. Is there anything you need? I probably should've asked a while ago and I'm sorry."

"No, no. I'm good." She takes her hand away from mine and takes a sip of her water. "Actually, I started volunteering down at Sandbridge. They have a surfing program for Gold Star families."

I chuckle. That's right. Riley used to move heaven and hell to have some time on the waves. Anytime she could get to Padre Island, she raced there. Even cutting class on occasion. "Sometimes I forget your love of surfing. Some of the guys surf. Taya's husband, in fact."

"You still haven't gotten into it, huh?"

I shrug. "Done it a couple of times, but not really my thing." I'm not entirely sure why. I love the water. Surfing is a little too out of my control for me to really enjoy it. Give me a hard run or a ropes course any day. Getting whipped up by a wave just to tame it? There are other things I like better.

Our food arrives and we both eat in a comfortable silence. For the first time in a while, I feel at ease with a woman. Most of my dates have had an uncomfortableness, a stiffness. Forced conversation and awkward pauses. But with Riley, it's easy to just sit and take in the atmosphere.

She seems comfortable as well. It's the first time we've eaten together that she hasn't picked at her food as if she was trying to decide whether or not to eat it. Guess the restaurant was a great choice since she seems to be eating without hesitation. She never used to be a picky eater. Maybe she developed some kind of food intolerance that she's not comfortable sharing. Riley was definitely the girl who never farted in front another person. I suppose it might have something to do with those scars. I'll ask, but not now. Now I just want to enjoy looking at my beautiful wife over plates of amazing food.

With my plate nearly empty, I sit back in my chair. "How often do you volunteer?"

She finishes chewing, then swallows before answering.

"Two days a week. But it's also weather dependent. Plus, I got a call back for some work-at-home opportunities. That will probably impact my availability."

That's news to me. "Didn't know you applied for a job." I keep my voice even, pleased that she's letting me in a bit more.

She fiddles with the fork in her hand. "I want something for myself. Work has been hard to come by. But these two companies are solid. Pay isn't much, but they offer benefits like insurance and a 401k."

My brows furrow. She has my insurance. Why would she need to be concerned about that? Something doesn't add up here. "My plan should cover everything you need."

Her eyes go wide for a second and she doesn't respond right away. "Oh, I, uh . . . I guess talking to the other wives and learning what happened to Jim and your other teammate . . . I figured having a backup plan wouldn't be a bad idea."

Fuck.

Of course. Riley heard about Lux. We still miss him. Visit his grave when we can. So stupid of me not to think my wife wouldn't be worried about the possibility I could die, especially when she has the kids of Gold Star families in front of her whenever she volunteers at the beach. Living breathing examples of why a military family might need for a backup plan.

She's right. Having a backup plan isn't a bad idea. Maybe it's something I need to think about some more for myself. For my son. For Riley.

They're my family and if something does happen to me, I want to make sure they're taken care of. But for now my job is to support Riley with whatever she needs. "So, when do you start?"

"I'm not sure which opportunity I should take. Both offer paid training and I have to take a look at what extra hardware I might need to buy before I can even start."

Bingo.

I reach across and grab her hand. "If you want to run both opportunities past me, I'm all ears. But either way, tomorrow we're going shopping. Whatever you need, we'll buy."

She blinks rapidly and opens her mouth to speak, but no words come out.

I hold up a hand. "You're offering to support me with the lawyer, so let me help you get settled. I want you to be happy."

Riley's face scrunches. "I don't want to impose, especially if we part ways at the end of—"

There's a lot I need to learn, a lot of places I must have failed at being a good family man in the past considering how everyone leaves me, but this I can do. "Regardless of whether or not we end up together for the long haul, it's the very least I can do. Truthfully, the computer equipment doesn't even compare to the help you are giving me when it comes to my son."

She nods. "Thank you."

For Riley, there's not much I wouldn't do to make her happy. Even if what makes her happy is eventually leaving me.

CHAPTER FIFTEEN

Riley

THE AROMA OF slightly singed pancakes floats up the stairs. I follow the scent down into the kitchen just in time to see Lucas fling a spatula into the sink.

When we got home from the restaurant the night before, we went right back to bed. To Lucas's bed. Maybe it was going to be our bed. Lucas was everything I remembered him being when we were in high school. Tender and passionate and generous in his lovemaking. He was something more now, though, too. He wasn't a boy anymore. He was a man, and he took possession of me like a man. I slept better than I had in weeks with his strong arms around me, his warmth by my side, the solid mass of him near me.

Standing in the doorway wearing nothing but the dress shirt I'd practically torn off him the night before, there was a throb at my very center remembering it. Everything I'd hoped for when I'd finally let him see my scars was coming true. Nothing that I dreaded seemed to be on the horizon.

Lucas still hasn't noticed me, and I take a moment to admire the man in action. Even just putting pancakes on a plate and balancing syrup and silverware in his hands, his movements are confident and sure. The muscles in his forearms, bunching and stretching. No part of this man isn't toned within an inch of its life. Something makes him shake his head as he works.

"What's going on in here?" I ask.

He spins around and the look he gives me spreads warmth all over my body, as sweet as the syrup he's carrying. "Figured I'd make us some breakfast so I can sit in the morning sunshine and look at my beautiful wife." He gestures with a nod toward the kitchen table and I follow, a little nervous about what kind of pancake he's made.

He sets the pancakes down. And they're just that. Pancakes. No chocolate chips or blueberries or bananas. Plain. I realize how closely he's been watching me and how hard he's trying to make things work.

"Let's eat," he says.

I turn and pick up the glasses sitting on the island and bring them over to the table, then sit down. I know we should talk about the night before, but I'm not sure how to start. I take the pitcher and fill my glass with water.

Lucas piles pancakes on his plate and slathers them with butter. I put a couple of them on my plate. When I look up, his eyes are on me. He chews slowly, his head tilted just a bit to the side as he watches me. "What are the scars from?"

Damn it. I drop my fork and groan. I'd started to hope that his acceptance of those scars the day before had meant I wouldn't have to go into detail. No such luck. "An appendectomy." Maybe I could get away with a scaled-down version of the truth.

He nods and eats a few more bites. I can practically hear the gears whirring in his head. "Graves had an appendectomy last year and has one little scar."

Panic flutters in my chest. When he'd kissed my scars and talked about how brave and strong I was, I felt more myself than I had in years. I want that so much. I want as much of it as I can get. As soon as he finds out the extent of what happened to me and what it could mean now, it'll be over. I want to savor a bit more of that feeling. Maybe I'll get approved for that new drug and won't have any more flare-ups. Then he'll never have to know about Riley the sick girl, Riley the weak girl, Riley who has to be handled with kid gloves. And Lisa will never have to know that I have a chronic health condition that might sometimes make it difficult for me to take care of Mason.

Fifteen years ago, I lied to him. Told him I didn't want to see him anymore. Even worse, I'd let my father tell him I didn't want to see him anymore and that it was because he didn't measure up. I'd hurt him with those lies and I'd hurt myself. It's time to put that behind me. It's time for me to come clean.

"Actually, I have Crohn's disease. All the surgeries actually did start with the appendectomy, but my symptoms got worse while you were away with your mom at that yoga seminar. I guess I had started showing some early signs of Crohn's for a while, but had ignored it. Figured it was nothing more than some cramps. I'd push through it."

He nods. "I know how you were back then. Pain was something to rise above, like that damn broken arm."

"Turns out that wasn't such a great plan. By the time I told anyone, my appendix had burst and I had to have emergency surgery." I push my plate of pancakes away. "It happens. Most people get better after surgery and some antibiotics. Some, however, don't."

Lucas stares at his plate, cutting his food into tiny bits as if trying to find some way to release his emotions. "And you were one of the ones who didn't get better?"

I blow out a breath. "Things went wrong. Really wrong. The pain. The cramping. The inability to hold on to food." He looks up at me. "It was . . . a mess. I needed help. Lots of it. It's why my father said you couldn't take care of me. He knew how much that would take."

He rolls his eyes. "Riley, that's bullshit. He had it set in his mind at least a year before that. He never came right out and said it, but he made enough comments that I knew. My family isn't rich. He wanted you to be with someone who had money. Always had. Nothing else really mattered to him."

I narrow my eyes. "It isn't just about you and me. You forget my older sister died when she was twelve. From a severe asthma attack. You're a parent. How would you feel, what would you have done or said if you had one child die from a medical emergency and then your other child got sick? You'd want to know that child would be with someone who could take care of them."

"I wouldn't have ripped someone else apart." His nostrils flair. "He was wrong too. I'm a good provider. I own a house and a car and I can buy my family everything they need. I've taken on second jobs and signed up for per diem opportunities. I've done everything I can to be sure my wife and child want for nothing. I've proven myself ten times over."

"You're not hearing me." I lean closer, my face heating. "This isn't about money. My parents wanted to make sure I was cared for medically. You were just a kid. How were you going to do that? You have no idea how bad it got."

"Of course I don't. You won't tell me anything." He tosses his fork down on his plate.

He has a point. I take a deep breath and blow it out and square my shoulders. "I had surgery after surgery. It kept getting worse. Then an infection set in. Eventually, I had an ileostomy and a colostomy."

His brow furrows and I clamp my lips shut tight. If only those words would never have had to pass my lips. Even so, they're just words and barely describe the physical and emotional devastation those months wreaked on me.

My husband remains quiet, just looks at me, giving me time to continue. And I do after slowly exhaling. "It was . . . horrible. I was lucky. They ended up not being permanent, but it was months and months of pain and sickness. I've been managing since then with watching my diet and some meds. Afterward, though, people treated me differently. My parents act like I'm a porcelain doll who has to be protected at all costs. I don't want to be viewed as the sick girl. I want the opportunity to prove myself. I want a chance to be myself. Riley. Not Riley, the Sick Girl."

My husband's jaw tics. "That's why you moved out this way? To get away from them?"

I shrug. "Pretty much. Except . . ." Do I tell him everything? Really lay it on the table?

"Except what?"

"It's why I broke up with you too. I know my dad did the actual deed, but I had to cut you lose, Luc. I know you. I know you would have given up everything to stay by my side, and I couldn't let that happen. You deserved to have a life."

His jaw tightens. "Should've let that be my decision."

"Couldn't, because I already knew what decision you'd make."

We stare at each other in silence for a moment, the stack of pancakes going cold between us. He drops his gaze first and clears his throat. "And how are you now? Are you okay?"

I cross my fingers in my lap under the table. "Sure. I have to be careful, but I'm doing great." Maybe if I say it enough, it will be true.

He picks up his fork and takes another bite of pancakes and chews, thinking. "Why'd you hide that from me now?"

The memory of the embarrassment and shame I felt watching someone walk out on me after finding out about my condition rushes over me. "Other people have decided they don't want to deal with someone who's chronically ill.

Or they treat me the way my parents do. Either way, it's always all about my illness. I'm more than Crohn's disease."

"Is there anything else I need to know?"

There is, but I'm not ready to talk about everything yet. He knows the most important part. I want to start my new meds—and hope they work so I can start feeling better—before laying everything else on him. Deep down, I'm still worried that if he finds out how bad things can get and how I joined the program for the medical benefits, he'll throw in the towel.

But there is something I can share, something he can help with. "Sometimes I have flare-ups and when that happens, I have to be on a strict diet. I watch what I eat anyway, but it's more intense. Sometimes I'll even lose a bit of weight because of it."

Lucas reaches across the table, squeezes my hand. "Thank you for sharing."

And that was it. No interrogation. No barrage of questions. No jumping up to throw out anything in the kitchen that I couldn't eat. Just a thank you for letting him in, for trusting him.

He leans back in his chair. "So, how about we look at what you need for your job?"

I nearly choke on the water I'm sipping, not having expected such a dramatic shift in topic. "Seriously? I, uh, have a list."

He smiles. "Of course you do."

My husband stands and starts clearing the table. If only I

could turn back time, have had more faith in him. Things might've turned out different. I shake the thought away because that would mean Mason might not exist. No, maybe this was the way it was meant to be all along.

Lucas heads back to the table and offers me his hand to help me to my feet. He places his hands on my hips and I stare into his eyes. Going backward isn't an option, but I can certainly adapt to the way we move forward. "Actually, I was also wondering if you could help me analyze the two job offerings I received. Not sure which one to go with."

A smile spreads across his face, the corners of his eyes wrinkling. "Happy to assist."

"Then we can have a snack." I wink, then let my gaze drop to his groin.

A deep growl fills the air around us, his pupils dilating instantaneously. "If you keep that up, we may not make it to the store."

I reach down and cup his dick. "No shopping, no snack. And I haven't tasted you in years. Don't wanna keep me waiting longer, do you?"

"No."

I pat him on the shoulder, then head for the stairs to shower as my husband just stands there, a massive bulge in his pants.

CHAPTER SIXTEEN

Lucas

MASON HELPS CARRY in the brown paper bags full of groceries. Luckily, Riley is out volunteering with the surf school, giving me enough time to surprise her with dinner. After she opened up to me about Crohn's, I decided to do some research. Not that I couldn't have asked Riley to tell me, but I didn't want to put her on the spot. I also didn't want her minimizing it. I knew what she was like. I hadn't forgotten her playing that soccer match with a broken arm.

It was a lot to take in and I don't ever recall noticing anything when we were growing up. Maybe that's why she dumped my ass. Because I never noticed, never bothered to make the extra effort. I shake my head and concentrate on the task at hand. "Okay, buddy. Are you going to help me cook too?"

Mason rolls his eyes. "Maybe just a little. But I promised Parker we would play video games for a bit."

I take in a big, slow breath. I swear part of me wants to chuck the console in the garbage. But now I don't even have a leg to stand on when colleges have eSports teams. Or the multi-million-dollar prize tournaments. Who would've thought gaming would become a profession?

Not me.

"You can play for a bit, but you did promise to help out."

Mason switches the bag of groceries to his other side. "Dad, I know, and I want to. Just not the cooking part."

"Fine."

Mason sets down the bag of food next to the stove and takes off. My son seems to be in better spirits when he's here, but there are still issues at school, ones he refuses to share with me or Lisa, no matter how many times we ask. If only the boy would communicate, maybe we'd be able to find a solution. Not sure how I can expect the kid to understand that when the adults around him are still struggling with it, though.

After placing the bags in my arms down on the counter, I grab my phone and open the ebook app. Two days ago I purchased some recipe books for ideas on what to cook that Riley would also be able to eat. Then I had the great idea of surprising her with a dinner made especially for her by me.

So far everything is going to plan. The store had fresh salmon and all the other ingredients that I need to make the avocado-pineapple salsa. The pictures in the ebook make the plate look mouthwatering. Hopefully, I can replicate it. I can cook, had to growing up, especially with both parents working more than one job. I also enjoy the idea of having someone to cook for. Though, I don't want to end up like

Stephens, always cooking for Taya.

I snort, imagining Taya attempting to help. She'd most likely end up rubbing her eyes after cutting up the jalapeño and onions. Not sure how Stephens manages. Taya has nearly set fire to the kitchen a couple of times, twice after giving birth to Otto. My teammate claims it's because his wife gets easily distracted by the baby, but I think Taya's just not cut out to cook. Lord help Stephens and Otto. The only thing that woman should make for dinner is reservations.

After setting out the ingredients on the counter and making sure the recipe is pulled up on the screen, I get to work. Surprisingly the salsa is easy to prepare and the salmon will go in the oven in about twenty minutes.

Just enough time to set up for a romantic evening.

After washing my hands, I grab the flowers I purchased and carry them into the dining room. This is the one room I love in the house. The space is grand, to say the least. The huge mahogany table takes up most of the vast area. I place the flowers in the center between two tall, silver candelabras holding smooth white candles.

Not sure when the fine china was last used, but tonight is as good as any holiday. Glad Lisa decided to leave it behind. Then again, with her upcoming wedding, I'm sure she'll get something newer. Once the table is set, I head back into the kitchen and preheat the oven. Time to get ready myself.

After running up the stairs and into my room, I strip down and take a quick shower, planning what to wear. Suit sounds good. Just as I turn off the water, the oven beeper goes off. Time to cook the salmon. Wrapping a towel around my waist, I rush back downstairs and place the fish inside the oven to cook.

"Mason, time to get ready!"

Yup, my son decided he wanted to be our server for tonight. Granted, there was a bribe involving a Big Mac, which he leapt at, since he's hardly ever allowed to eat fast food.

As I reach the stairs to head up to my room, Mason comes barreling up from the den. "What am I wearing?"

"Whatever you want."

He frowns. "Well, what are you wearing?"

"A suit."

Mason frowns. "I only have one, and it's at Mom's."

I chuckle. "How about you wear a polo shirt and some khaki shorts?"

He nods and pushes past me, bounding up the stairs to his room. I follow, but turn right when I reach his door to get back to my room. Our room. The room Riley and I now share every night. The room where I fall asleep and wake up with her in my arms.

As I pull the suit from the closet from next to a row of her dresses, I spot my reflection. "Fucking hair is a mess."

Just one other thing to do. No big deal. After a few minutes with a blow dryer, some gel, and a brush, my hair is perfect. Now to get dressed.

Thank God everything is ironed and I don't have to add that to the list. Once my tie is in place and my jacket is buttoned, I head back downstairs and into the kitchen to check on the fish. A few more minutes and it will be done.

The front door closes. "Hello. I'm home."

"Dad, she's here."

"Mason, don't you look cute," I hear Riley say from the other room.

"Wait until you see my dad." The pride in his voice spreads a smile on my face.

A moment later Riley walks into the kitchen, takes in me in my suit and the dinner that's underway with her mouth agape. "What's going on?"

I walk over to place a kiss on her cheek. "Cooking my wife dinner."

Her expression is blank for a second, then she giggles. The sound is like music to me. "Really? You didn't have to do that."

"Wanted to." I spin her around and gently push her out of the kitchen, swatting her ass when she takes a step. "Go get ready. Food's almost done."

She must be excited, based on the little prance she does. While my wife freshens up, I grab the plates, then add the food to them. "Mason, remember, when you bring these in, do it one at a time. And be careful."

"I know. I know. The dishes are super expensive. I remember Mommy telling me." He rolls his eyes the same way that Riley does and somehow that makes my smile even bigger.

After tousling his hair, I grab the bottle of Dr. Hermann from the fridge. The Riesling should go well with the fish.

Had it before and it is one of my favorite—semisweet with a hint of pineapple.

Once the bottle is popped open, I fill our glasses. Mason wants to be in charge of the pitcher of water, so the second glass remains empty.

A few minutes later, Riley comes into the dining room wearing some kind of silky coral dress with a neckline that plunges down, leaving an exposed strip of skin that has my mouth watering at the idea of pressing my lips to it. Her blond hair cascades around her shoulders, her blue eyes sparkle, and her skin has a glow to it as if happiness is radiating from her. I know it's not just her time at the beach making her look that way and the thought of giving her that glow makes me puff out my chest a bit.

And fuck, do I want to forget about dinner and head back upstairs to bury myself deep in her. That'll make her glow. But Mason is here, and I didn't cook this dinner to let it spoil on the counter.

I clear my throat and rein my libido back in. "You are breathtaking."

"Not so bad yourself." She bites her bottom lip as her gaze roams over me, halting momentarily at the semi-growing bulge between my legs. "Looks like I have an idea about what may be for dessert."

While her words heat my blood, they also remind me of the fact there was something I forgot. Dessert. Scratching the back of my head, I shoot her a sheepish grin. "Hope it'll do since anything truly edible isn't on the menu. Sort of slipped my mind."

She leans in and bites my earlobe. "It'll do."

Sucking in a breath, I lead her over to where she will be sitting before I end up throwing her on the table to make her my main course. Once she is situated, I take a seat myself.

Riley stares at me, a questioning look on her face. "Um, I know you have a plan and all, but . . . where's the food?"

No sooner does she finish the sentence when Mason comes in carrying her plate. "Good evening. I will be your server for tonight. Today's special is . . . Dad, what is this?"

The corners of my mouth lift into a grin so wide, my teeth must be showing. I can't help it. My son is the best. He fills my heart with such joy. "Salmon with avocado-and-pineapple salsa."

He turns back to Riley. "Fish with salsa."

Riley busts out laughing and takes the plate. "Thank you, sir."

Mason nods, then runs off into the kitchen, reappearing a few seconds later with my food. Instead of the politeness Riley got, he plops the dish down in front of me, sending some pieces of pineapple bouncing onto the table.

"That will be deducted from your tip, young man."

He stops mid-stride. "Wait. You were paying me?"

"Yeah, right." If he were getting paid, that money would go directly to Inara for all the things my son and my best friend have broken of hers. Seriously, Martinez is the worst babysitter. "Now, go back to the kitchen and eat your own dinner."

"Okay." Mason turns to Riley. "Do you want some water before I go?"

"Sure, that will be great."

He shoots her a thumbs-up, then grabs the pitcher off the buffet and fills her glass. He then fills mine and places the pitcher back where he found it. He leaves the room after giving us both a deep bow.

Riley slaps the table, full-on snort-laughing. "Oh my God, where did that kid get his sense of humor from? Certainly not you."

"Tony. Hangs out way too much with him."

Riley picks up her fork and digs into the meal. I wait, wanting to know what she thinks. Her eyes close as she chews. "This is *so* good. You have to give me the recipe."

My muscles relax a bit. Finally did something right. "Found it in a book of recipes for people with Crohn's."

Riley jerks her head in my direction. "You . . . got a book of what to cook? For me?"

I nod.

She blinks rapidly, but I catch how her eyes grow wet. Definitely did the right thing.

We eat while we chat about her day and some of the kids she worked with. I fill her in on my day, at least what I'm allowed to tell her. Mason comes in and checks on us every so often. This time when he pops in, he runs over and gives me a hug, then turns to Riley. "Wanna play video games when you are done eating?"

"Maybe, but I'm not sure what your dad has planned."

"He's gotta clean up." Mason turns to me, the most evil smirk on his face. "I can't because I might break the expensive plates."

Yup, definitely influenced by my best friend. Martinez is going to hear about this. "Why don't you go set Riley's game up? She'll be down once we're done."

Mason nods and runs off.

"Hope you don't mind. Haven't seen my son this happy since he and Lisa moved out. He's almost like his old self." My throat tightens. If only I could fix whatever is going on with him, make it so he's always this happy.

Riley takes my hand in hers. "Moving had to have been tough. I'm sure being back here makes him feel comfortable. It's where he grew up. Maybe he just needs a little more time to adjust to his new school and for them to adjust to him."

"You're probably right."

We go back to eating, but my thoughts drift back to my son. I love him with all my heart. If I'd been around more, instead of being gone so much on deployments and for training, Mason might still live here. Lisa might not have left. I swallow hard, forcing the fish I'd been chewing past the growing knot in my throat.

Going forward, I vow to do better by my son. I have to. And from how much he's taken to Riley, that means making sure I do right by her as well.

CHAPTER SEVENTEEN

Riley

THIS ONLINE TRAINING is boring as hell. I seriously can't wait for it to be over. I click on the next module and the speaker begins talking. Okay, time to concentrate and take notes. There's a quiz at the end and I need to pass it. No way am I going to sit through this again.

My phone buzzes.

Lucas. A smile spreads across my face. I look forward to hearing his voice. The past weeks have been amazing. I didn't think it was possible to feel this happy.

I tap the talk button and put the call on speaker so I can continue writing. "Hi, handsome."

"Hey, Cupcake. Listen, I need to ask you a favor."

This can't be good. He knows I've got online training for the new job. He wouldn't ask unless there really wasn't another choice. "What's up?"

"Running late at work. Mason has a parent-teacher conference in a bit. I was supposed to head over there, find out what's been going on and see if the school had any ideas on how to help Mason adjust." Lucas goes silent for a moment, then his sigh echoes through the speaker. "Would you mind going?"

All the reasons not to do this come flooding in. A soft panic settles in that can grow or fade depending on what I do next. Mason isn't my child and God only knows how Lisa will react because sure as shit the teacher will mention my presence to her.

"Riley?"

"Sorry." I let out a shaky breath. "You think it will be okay? Like there won't be any bad repercussions with the custody battle?"

"Honestly, I think I'm screwed either way."

My heel bounces against the wood floor. Ugh, this shouldn't be so hard. I hate being stuck in the middle. "Sure. It's about Mason at the end of the day."

"Thank you. I'll text you the address and time."

Lucas hangs up and I turn my attention back to the laptop. The module has paused and is waiting for me to answer a question. At least the answer is clear as day for anyone with a bit of common sense.

After I answer, I save my place and get up from the couch. Time to get ready since the elementary school is about forty minutes away. Plus, Mason will be waiting since he's staying with us for the week. Guess this is what life being married to someone in Special Forces is like. It's not like Inara, Tara, and Marge didn't warn me. Expect the unexpected.

My phone dings. The address pops up in the alert on the

screen. Let's see how long the ride is going to be. After a few quick taps with my finger, my pulse picks up speed.

Of course, there's traffic. Murphy's freakin' Law. I have to be there in a little over an hour and the phone says it's going to take that long to get there.

Dropping the phone back down onto the couch, I head upstairs to quickly change, fix my hair, and brush my teeth. No way do I want to be the person with bad breath at this meeting.

Crap. Crap. Crap.

What does a person wear to one of these things?

I grab a pair of dark blue jeans and a button-down peach shirt. Next, fix hair. Ponytail should do. Spritz some perfume. Apply some lip gloss and mascara and I'm all set. Presentable. Neat. Not trying too hard.

I grab my phone, purse, and keys, then race to the car, just so I can sit in bumper-to-bumper traffic twenty minutes later with my hand going from tapping the steering wheel to hitting it as my anxiety rises. Where are all these people going, anyway? Can't they see I need to get somewhere?

Eventually the traffic subsides and my heart slows as the car picks up speed. I do some deep breathing and end up pulling into the parking lot with a few minutes to spare. The brick building in front of me is multi-storied. Behind it is a huge field with a playground, a basketball court, and a baseball field along with lots of wide-open grassy areas to run around in.

I stop for a second. Kids don't know how good they have

it. Or at least I didn't when I was their age. Things used to be so easy back then. The only worries were report cards and friends, and friends could be made by trading lunch snacks, far easier than when you're an adult.

I pull on the wood doors to the school, but they're locked. On my right is a doorbell and I press the button. There is a buzz a few seconds later and I pull the door and walk inside. A few short steps into the building and I'm met by a young woman with a bored expression on her face sitting behind a desk.

"How can I help you?"

"Uh, I'm here for a parent-teacher conference for Mason Craiger."

"Do you know what teacher you're supposed to see?" She opens a log book on her desk.

I pull out my phone. Crap. Lucas didn't give me that info. "No, I'm sorry I don—"

"Riley!!"

I spin around to find Mason running toward me. He gives me a big hug, his arms circling my waist. I lean down to plant a kiss on top of his head and inhale the smell of new-mown grass and little boy shampoo. "Hey, there. Dad sent me because he got stuck at work."

"Ma'am, who's the teacher you're seeing?" The woman behind the desk asks again, sounding unimpressed with my lack of knowledge and Mason's happiness at seeing me.

Mason looks at the lady. "Mrs. Shapiro, ma'am."

The woman nods. "May I have your license? Please sign

in. It will be room 201. Second floor." She turns the log book around so I can sign my name, then add my address and phone number.

My license too? Security is a hell of a lot different than when I went to school. This wasn't the time to argue, though. I hand the woman what she asks for and fill out the sign-in sheet. Once complete, she hands me a sticker badge with my name on it. "You can pick up your license on the way out."

I nod and then Mason grabs my hand and pulls me off down the hall. The school is big and spread-out, with wide, locker-lined hallways. Posters and student work and pictures of kids playing sports and performing in a play cover the walls. Some of the kids look huge.

"How old are those kids?" I ask, pointing to one that looks like he might have the start of a mustache.

Mason laughs. "Sixth graders."

We walk up the staircase and down the hall toward the back of the building. Then Mason turns into classroom 201. The room is bright and faces the field I'd seen behind the school. Rays of sunlight stream into the room through the massive windows. The desks are arranged in groups of six. Against the back wall is a library of books and at the front, in the center, a big whiteboard is mounted on the wall. Off to the side is the teacher's desk. A dark-haired woman in her fifties is seated behind it, looking through a stack of blue folders.

Schools definitely have changed.

"Mrs. Shapiro, this is my stepmom," Mason says.

I freeze. What did he just call me? The woman in front of me smiles and I have to force myself to move forward.

Stepmom.

I know that's what I am legally, but a piece of paper wouldn't mean anything if Mason didn't think of me that way. The word pierces my heart, flooding my chest with a warmth I've never felt. Yeah, this day has been full of surprises. Good ones, for a change.

Mrs. Shapiro stands up and extends her hand. "Good afternoon. Mrs. Craiger, is it?"

"Yes." I shake the teacher's hand, then take a seat. "Lucas couldn't make it, but we wanted to make sure someone was here for Mason."

"Yes, Ms. Ellis did inform me that Mason would be staying with his father for the week." Mrs. Shapiro sits back down.

Ellis? Oh, must be Lisa's surname.

"Anyway, I'm glad you're here." Mrs. Shapiro opens a blue file folder and pulls out examples of Mason's work. "Mason, why don't you go work on your writing project on the computer?"

He nods and heads off to an area of the classroom that has five desktops. This school has everything.

"As you can see, your stepson is quite an exceptional young man. His scores are excellent and he's a good writer. His Lexile scores are above grade level and he doesn't have any issues with math."

I look over the work. Mason is smart. Takes after his father. "This is great news. I'm sure my husband will be proud of him." I know I am. I look over to where he's sitting at the computer, absorbed in whatever project he's working on.

"Mason does have a problem, though." Mrs. Shapiro leans back in her chair and narrows her eyes a bit. "With his classmates. The school administration and I had hoped it would get better, but it has not."

That doesn't sound good. "What kind of problem?"

Mrs. Shapiro presses her lips together until they're not much more than a straight line and then says, "Mason has been getting into fights with the other students."

"Physically?" Definitely not good and possibly above my pay grade here.

Mrs. Shapiro nods her head. "We have had some altercations during recess. Ms. Ellis has been called a few times and the principal has spoken with her, but Mason isn't getting any better. The other day, he overreacted to something another student said and disrupted the entire lesson." The look on her face tells me she's still pissed about it.

My head tilts sideways the slightest bit and I recall what Mason told me that day we played video games with his friend, about how he was being teased in ways that were truly cruel. My stomach sinks. He didn't tell his mother. He only told me. He's got no one else in his corner.

Which means, now it's time to keep the vow I made and stand up for my stepson. "Mrs. Shapiro, have you spoken to the other students involved in these altercations?"

She looks taken aback. "What do you mean? Mason is always the instigator. The other children know the classroom rules and that we expect them to be respectful."

Can she really not know what's happening in her own classroom? Or does she just not care? I definitely am not going to stand for the implication that Mason isn't respectful. "It's my understanding that the other students are not being respectful to Mason. Are you aware of the things they say to him?"

Mrs. Shapiro straightens in her chair while fidgeting with the file folder. "Yes, I've heard that they accuse Mason of fabricating."

Fabricating? Is that what she calls it? But that tells me she does know and isn't doing anything to help Mason, and that is one hundred percent unacceptable to me. "Mrs. Shapiro, they claim he's lying about his father's service. They say that Lucas actually abandoned Mason. Lucas is in the military and leaves for long periods of time to protect our country. We don't always know where he's going or how long he'll be gone because of security concerns. You are aware of this, correct?" I pin her with a stare, eyes narrowed to make sure she understands I'm not some pushover.

"Ms. Ellis mentioned it."

I sit back and cross my arms in front of my chest. "Well, what are you doing to protect Mason? Because from the bits he mentions to me, it isn't much. Do you have other students whose parents are in the military? Any services you offer those children?"

Mrs. Shapiro squirms and avoids eye contact. "There are a few students. We do have them meet with the counselor if there is a problem. She has even met with Mason a few times."

"Good. That's a start." I lean forward. "But helping Mason is only half the problem. What are you doing about the other kids?"

"Mrs. Craiger, I assure you we're not putting all the blame on Mason." Mrs. Shapiro leans forward, too, but I'm not backing down.

"Sure sounds that way to me."

She stands up and huffs. "Maybe it's better if I speak with Ms. Ellis once she gets back."

"You go do that." I grab my purse and stand. "Hey, Mason. Save what you're doing and let's get out of here."

He looks over his shoulder and nods. Then looks at his teacher, who is all flustered, then back to me. A shit-eating grin spreads across his face. Poor kid needs someone fighting for him, and I'm happy to be that someone.

Once Mason logs off and grabs his book bag, we head toward the door. Before we walk out, I stop and turn to look back at his teacher. "Oh, I was just thinking. It might be a good idea for me, my husband, and Lisa to meet with the principal. Maybe even the school board to discuss the matter further. I'm sure they would be interested in how children of military personnel are being treated in your classroom."

Mrs. Shapiro's mouth falls agape. I offer a little wave, then exit. No one is going to mess with my family and expect me to idly stand by.

CHAPTER EIGHTEEN

Lucas

IT'S BEEN OVER a week since I eavesdropped on Riley talking to Mason's teacher. I still can't get over the way Riley stood up for Mason. At the last minute, our training op was canceled. I hightailed it to the school, hoping to get there in time to be at the conference. Heard Riley's raised voice from down the hall. My first instinct had been to run in there and back her up, but then I remembered what she'd said about her parents treating her like she couldn't take care of herself. In there with Mrs. Shapiro, Riley had sounded strong and confident and able to take on the world. Wouldn't want to take that from her for anything.

Plus, it sounded like she knew some things about my son I wasn't aware of myself.

So, I stepped inside the empty classroom next door and listened instead. Listened to how she'd totally told the teacher off. The part that bothers me is I'm not sure I would have done the same. Mason hadn't shared what had been going on with me. He hadn't trusted me with that information. Without having all the information, maybe I would've sided with Mrs. Shapiro.

And that breaks my heart.

I lift the glass of water in my hand and take a sip, looking out the living room window. No matter how hard I try to concentrate on something else, like the landscapers across the street, I can't help but further analyze the situation. The more I do, the more I realize how out of touch I am with Mason. With his life. And that means second-guessing myself as a father.

If only I could be more like Riley. She doesn't know Mason that well, but she acted more like a parent in that moment than I ever have. Glad I got to see it too.

"You okay?"

Riley's voice pulls me from my thoughts, and I turn around to face her where she stands in the doorway. "Um, yeah."

"You don't look completely okay." She studies me, concentrating on my face. "Wanna talk about it?"

I walk over and place a kiss on her forehead and wrap my arms around her, inhaling the lilac scent of her shampoo. One thing about my wife, she's perceptive. Always has been. Maybe that's why Mason felt comfortable telling her about what his classmates had been saying. Also, growing up together meant she knew all my expressions. Most of them, anyway. Not much I can hide from her when she catches me off guard. "Well, I, uh, heard the way you handled Mrs. Shapiro."

Riley steps back and meets my gaze, hands against my

chest. "You were there? Why didn't you come in?" A faint pink stains her cheeks.

"Seemed like you had everything under control." And then some.

She places her hands on her hips and I miss the contact with her instantly. "Then why didn't you meet up with us after?"

I rub the back of my neck. Not sure what to say. There were so many reasons I'd ducked into the classroom next door. "Because you and Mason seemed to be bonding and I didn't want to intrude."

Riley purses her lips into a pretty pink O, gaze still locked with mine. "I guess that makes sense. Still, you could've told me later on that day instead of waiting a week."

"True. But I also needed to figure out how to diffuse the situation when Lisa finds out." I wasn't sure Lisa was going to be as impressed and thrilled about how Riley handled the situation as Mason and I were.

"Has she said anything?" she asks.

"No." Which means my ex-wife hadn't spoken to the teacher yet, nor has my son mentioned what happened. There also haven't been any more reports of Mason acting out in school. Wouldn't be surprised if Mason senses some tension between his mother and Riley. He's a perceptive one too. Probably doesn't want to stir the pot.

Riley returns to me and runs a finger down my chest, and a line of heat follows her touch. "Well, thank you for giving me the opportunity to bond with your son. I'm crazy about him."

I press my lips to her ear and give her a light kiss. "And thank you for defending him. You were a great mom in there."

"Really?" The pink stain is back on her cheeks and her voice lilts a bit higher. The look in her eyes speaks of both joy and uncertainty. I can tell how much pride she takes in the idea of being a good mom to Mason. I can't imagine anything that would make me love her more.

"Yes," I say and hope she understands how much I mean it.

Riley nuzzles into me, standing up on her toes to place a kiss on my cheek, but she doesn't stop there. Soon lips and teeth graze over my neck. I pull away the slightest bit. "Where's this coming from?"

"Just feeling confident, and all that praise deserves a nice reward." There's a fire in her eyes that I recognize, and my breath quickens in response. She takes the glass from my hand and sets it down on the coffee table. I love that fire. Love the way she stands tall, like nothing could stop her.

With a palm on my chest, she backs me up to the couch, then pushes me down. Holding my gaze, she lowers herself down in front of me until she's on her knees, fingernails scratching hard enough for me to feel it on my thighs through my jeans.

"Fuck, Riley . . ."

I hold her hair back from her face to get a better view of that fresh pink rosiness of her cheeks that is getting more and more intense with every passing second.

She undoes my belt and rips the leather from my belt loops. Every single fiber in my body wants to pick her up, throw her over my shoulder, then haul ass to the bedroom. My bedroom. I want to drop her onto the bed, get her under me, and growl about how beautiful she is as she comes.

But this is Riley, and one thing I know from our past is that once she has her mind set on something, there is no changing it. Not that I'm about to complain.

She nuzzles into my hard-on from outside my pants. Her eyes flutter shut as she increases the pressure, driving her cheekbone into the sensitive underside, compressing the shaft and pressing against my balls with her chin. Using her tongue, she traces around the outline of my cock, paying special attention to the ridge and the head.

Looking up again, she keeps her eyes locked with mine, as if to make sure I'm watching. She licks her lips, opens her mouth, and then she takes my jean-clad shaft between her teeth and very lightly bites down on my cock.

"Holy fucking hell," I growl as my head falls back so I'm looking up at the ceiling. The desire in that bite felt incredible. Her teeth put the right pressure in all the right places, doing exactly the thing I didn't know I needed until right this minute.

She does it again, lower this time, sending a surge of fire through my spine. When I hiss and my hips buck, she stops. But only to unfasten the button of my jeans and pull down the zipper. I swallow hard and watch her. My heart pounds in my chest. In my throat. In my cock. Everywhere.

She licks up the underside of the shaft and positions my hands on the couch cushion, keeping them wide on either side of me. "Those stay there. We clear?"

"Anything you say." My voice is gravelly, deep, and filled with a need so ferocious, I'm unsure if I'll be able to control it.

"Touch me and I'll stop." She licks a long, wet line up the left side of the shaft, encircles the head, then goes back down again.

It isn't going to be easy, but she has me, literally, by the balls. She takes me deep into her throat and I grow harder. My breaths quicken and become shallow, the muscles in my neck tense and tighten.

"Fuck, Riley." My fingers dig into the cushion as I try to find something solid to hold on to.

When she goes back down to the base and teases my balls, lingering at the spot where they meet the shaft, I damn near lose my mind, but she isn't done. Not by a long shot, and I'm not sure how much longer I can hold on.

The moment she draws my balls back into her mouth, I slap the couch with all the force I can muster, sucking in a breath through my nose. That doesn't help. Neither does gritting my teeth.

She sucks me deeper. And deeper. Not letting up for a moment. And the more I groan and moan, the more my hips buck involuntarily, the more incessant she becomes.

"Riley . . . can't take much . . . more."

She holds the base with both hands and flicks her tongue along the underside, moving up to the tip and teasing the opening very gently. "Riley, now. I'm gonna come."

She doesn't get off. Instead, she sucks me harder, keeping the head of my cock on her tongue. My arms fly backward and I grab the back of the couch as I arch and widen my legs, holding on for dear life.

I suck in a hard breath and hold it as my orgasm rips through me. Every nerve ending in my body fires off, every muscle contracting. The intensity is so powerful my ears begin to ring.

As my orgasm fades, Riley releases my still twitching dick from her mouth. And I finally exhale. She straddles me and places a gentle kiss on my lips. "I forgot how much I enjoyed getting you off."

That makes the both of us. But I don't say that, mostly because I'm still trying to catch my breath.

One thing is for certain . . . the more time passes, the more I realize Riley is the perfect match for me.

I hope with all my heart she feels the same way because I'm not sure I can handle her leaving me again.

CHAPTER NINETEEN

Riley

MARGE'S BACKYARD IS incredible. The air is filled with the fragrance of lavender from the garden. She claims the flowers are a natural bug repellent, especially for mosquitoes. More impressive is the koi pond, a little oasis surrounded with rocks and ferns. Sunlight, filtered through the leaves of a sweet bay magnolia tree, sparkles before my eyes. Five beautiful orange-and-white fish glide through the water, swishing and swirling about each other as if going through the motions of some kind of ancient dance. They're mesmerizing. I can't imagine how Marge takes care of this all by herself most days. It can't be easy.

The air is warm and soft. May is nearly over, which means spring is coming to a close. Summer heat and humidity will soon fill the air, making the ocean a refuge for many. Not that I mind. I absolutely love the ocean. Just not the crowds.

The shrieks of children capture my attention. Amongst them are Mason and Marge's younger daughter Leslie, who happens to be the birthday girl. Jim and Bear are also in the mix. I chuckle at the sight of two grown Navy SEALs wrestling with a bunch of little kids, but the two men are in their glory. Maybe Jim isn't such a bad guy after all. I'm beginning to see what Taya sees in him as he rolls around in the grass with children clinging to him.

Speaking of SEALs . . . I stand and spin around, trying to see where my husband is. Oh, no. Guess I'm about to get firsthand experience with the chaos Lucas and Tony have a reputation for creating.

"Mira, Riley." Inara comes up from behind me. Her black hair is pulled up off her neck in a messy bun and a floral sundress swirls around her legs. "These two fools might ruin this party."

All I see are two grown men hiding behind the bouncy house until Inara tugs me close and points to Tony's hands. Oh, hell. They're going to egg Jim and Bear. Seriously? I look at Inara, not sure what will happen next. "How bad is this going to be?"

"Wouldn't be surprised if someone ended up with a broken nose. Maybe a black eye or two." Inara pulls out her phone, taps on the screen, then puts the phone to her ear. "Taya, you better get out here. Tony and Lucas are about to stir shit up. You know how pissy Jim can get."

I can't make out what Taya says, but Inara tucks the phone back into her pocket a few seconds after speaking. Of course, the moment we return our attention back to the possible future crime scene, my gaze falls on a white oval object sailing through the air.

My mouth falls open when it hits Jim in the back of the head. Of course I didn't see which dolt threw it, only that Lucas and Tony have tucked themselves farther behind the inflatable as they laugh and slap each other on the back.

"What the fuck?" Jim spins around, searching for the culprit. Yellow goo oozes down the back of his head.

"Watch your mouth," Taya chides from the back door of Marge's house.

As soon as he focuses on his wife, another curse cuts through the air. This time from Bear. Yup. He got egged too. He reaches back and wipes at the mess on his neck, then shakes his hand to try to get the slop off.

Tony and Lucas double over with laughter. "Uh, Inara, how many eggs do they have?" I ask.

She groans. "I think I saw one of those eighteen-egg cartons."

That's a lot of egg-shaped chaos to wreak. Maybe we should intervene before it gets out of hand. "Do we rat them out?"

She gives me a look. "Do you want to die?"

Nope. I shake my head and stand back to watch the scene unfold. Jim is beet red and I swear there's steam coming out of his ears. Mason is rolling on the ground laughing as Leslie picks up remnants of sticky eggshells and throws them at her dad. Oh, wonderful. The kids think this is a great game.

"Martinez! Craiger!" Bear barrels toward the bouncy house as my husband takes off running toward the back door.

Holy crap. Lucas is fast. Faster than I remember. But so is Bear and I'm surprised by that, considering how big and burly the man is. Guess I shouldn't make assumptions about people's capabilities based on appearance.

While Bear chases after my husband, Jim sets his sights on Tony. Inara huffs beside me. "This was supposed to be a kid's party. I forgot Lucas and Anthony are the biggest children of them all."

I laugh. "What's going to happen if you do have kids?"

She huffs and points to her husband using her entire hand. "I already have one. Right there."

I tilt my head sideways, brows furrowed. "Never seen that gesture before."

Inara glances at her hand and snorts. "Tony does it all the time when he's mad or very passionate. Think it's called a knife hand. God help me. Wonder what other mannerisms I've adopted from Tony."

My attention returns to my husband. It's fun seeing this side of him, watching as he interacts with the men on his team. The ones he fights alongside, that count as his brothers. His family.

Part of me is jealous because I want that kind of camaraderie in my life. My illness has isolated me from friends. I thought I'd made peace with it, but maybe not. Then I watch Jim throw himself at Tony, tackling the other man to the ground. Okay, I don't want that exact kind of camaraderie.

"Jim Stephens, I swear to God if you throw one punch in front of the children, you will be sleeping in the backyard for the rest of your life." Taya is not just pointing at her husband, but doing the knife-hand point Inara just did moments ago, eyes blazing. If I were Jim, I'd do what she says. She doesn't look like she brooks any nonsense at all.

"Sorry, sorry. Ouch!" Lucas's voice emanates from inside the house and my eyes move from Taya to the door behind her.

A couple of seconds later, Marge emerges, leading Lucas out the door. I can't help but laugh. She's a petite woman, maybe five feet, and she's dragging my six-foot-two husband around by the ear. He's bent over at the waist, shuffling after her and begging for mercy.

"Marge, I'm sorry," Lucas protests. "Look, it was Tony's idea."

Inara and I walk over to where all four men and Marge are gathered. Though my feet start dragging the closer I get, because the expression on Marge's face is scary to say the least. Yet, surrounding the adults are laughing children who have their mouths covered as if they could hide their amusement.

"You two are lucky I don't beat you to death. Considering you kept your shenanigans outside and nothing broke in the house, I'll let it slide." Marge releases Lucas's ear and pokes him and Tony in their chests as she speaks. "But the jokes stop now. You want to play games that lead to you dolts getting your butts kicked, do it on base. Not at my house. Capisce?"

"Yes, ma'am," the two say in unison.

Marge turns to Jim and Bear. "And you two, drop it. It's over. I don't want to hear another word about getting egged. Get over it."

Jim grunts while Bear huffs, neither man uttering a word.

"Everyone go get cleaned up. It's almost time to eat." Marge turns and marches back inside.

Inara and I follow to help her set up. Hayden, Marge and Bear's oldest daughter who just got home from college, pulls some bowls from the refrigerator and hands them to us. We carry them to the tables set up outside. There's a large bowl of tricolored pasta salad, complete with tomatoes and feta cheese. There is also a vegetable salad with diced tomatoes, cucumbers, and green bell peppers mixed in olive oil. Another bowl contains herb-roasted squash.

Tony walks in to grab the potatoes and corn for Bear to cook on the barbeque. Peeking out the window, I spot Marge's husband with Lucas standing next to him, all the animosity from the egging completely gone. Since everything is pretty much set up, I head outside and make my way over to him.

The smell of barbeque ribs floods my nose. If only I could partake the way I want to. But that would mean dealing with the repercussions, including inflaming my GI tract. Not something I'm willing to do. The risk isn't worth the reward. I've learned that the hard way.

When I reach my husband, I wrap my arms around him. "Hey there, handsome. Glad to see you made it out of the egging fiasco in one piece."

He chuckles and Bear glares at him before turning to me. "Riley, how cooked do you want your salmon? Or do you want chicken burgers instead?"

My brows furrow. "You guys eat chicken burgers? Thought this was a red meat and potatoes gang."

Lucas wraps his arm around my waist. "Called Bear yesterday to make sure there would be food you were able to eat."

What. The. Hell.

My pulse thunders in my ears. Please, God, tell me I heard this man wrong. That he didn't make some big deal about my condition to the hosts of a party we're attending. My heart sinks as it all starts to make sense. Salmon. Chicken burgers. Those side dishes. I feel so exposed, like I'm standing naked in front of these people, and Lucas is the one who stripped me bare.

I remove myself from his embrace and shake my head. I knew this would happen. I trusted him and he has wasted no time in betraying me. My nostrils flare. "Can I talk to you?" I try to keep my tone even, but I'm failing.

Lucas eyes me suspiciously, then follows as I walk away from his teammate. When we are a safe distance away from other guests, I spin around and glare at my husband, eyes narrowed to mere slits. "Why would you say anything to them about what I can and can't eat? Why would you tell them about my condition?"

My husband takes a step back. "Because I wanted to make sure you could enjoy the party. I was trying to help."

"Without asking me? Without letting me know?" I close the distance between us and poke him in the chest the way Marge had, but with less good humor. He's doing it. I should have known he wouldn't be able to help himself. He's overstepping. Going too far. Not letting me handle my business the way I choose. "What you should have done was speak to me first before putting my information on blast to your friends. It's a breach of *my* privacy. I decide when people get to know about my medical condition. Not you. There are reasons I don't tell many people about it."

He goes to place a hand on my shoulder but I pull away. "Riley—"

I hold up a hand. "No, shut it. I don't want to hear an apology. What you did . . . do you understand how much I don't want people treating me differently? Seeing me as the sick girl who has to get special treatment?"

My gaze drops to the ground. He broke my trust. Ruined the dream I had of people seeing me as normal. Tears prick at the corners of my eyes. It's worse than that. Based on my husband's actions, that's how *he* sees me. As another person for him to take care of. Like I can't do it myself. I can't even pick and choose what I'm going to eat without help. Once again, I'm the sick girl.

The one Goddamn thing I didn't want in all of this.

Without saying another word, I turn on my heel, say a

quick goodbye to Marge, Hayden, Inara and Taya, grab my things, and head to the car. So much for enjoying the day. How quickly life changes.

CHAPTER TWENTY

Lucas

I STAND ON the driveway rubbing the base of my neck and watch as Riley drives away. I'm not getting it. I mean, sure, she's pissed. Hella pissed, as a matter of fact. Even though she told me why, I still don't understand. I was trying to help. I've seen how careful Riley is at home and restaurants with her meals and, after doing some research, I understood the minefield a barbeque might present for her. I also know how much she does not want to be fussed over. By doing a little advance work, I'd tried to remove those mines for her, help her navigate the barbeque and make it into a more successful mission for both of us.

Instead, it blew up in my face. *Got it wrong again, Craiger. As per usual.* Can't even learn from my mistake, either, since I don't understand why what I did was so damn wrong. What was I supposed to do? Nothing? The least a man can do is make sure there's a roof over his wife's head and food in her belly, and I want to do way more than the least for Riley. Plus, a SEAL doesn't keep information from his team. We live as a team and die as a team.

I'm still standing there, looking at the empty road, when Graves pulls into the parking spot Riley pulled out of.

"What's up, Lucas?" he asks as he gets out of his Ford Explorer with a bottle of wine and flowers in his hands. He looks where I'm looking, trying to figure out what I'm staring at, which is a whole lot of empty road.

I shrug and gesture with my head toward the backyard. "Team's back there."

Graves gives his shirt a little tug and nods. "On your six."

I walk into the backyard in front of him.

Everyone is gathered around the table and the grill. Marge throws me some side-eye and looks over at Taya, who angles herself so her back is to me. Hayden looks up from putting silverware out on the table and shakes her head, her hair a pink-and-purple waterfall. Inara crosses her arms over her chest, muttering something under her breath that sounds suspiciously like "idiota."

How am I an idiot? I made a point of educating myself and my team.

Bear, Stephens and Martinez all watch me. I walk back over to them while Graves walks over to the table and hands the bottle of wine to Marge and the bouquet to Hayden.

"Thank you," Marge says. "How sweet."

"My stepparents said I shouldn't ever come to a party with my hands swinging free."

"Well, it wasn't necessary, but I appreciate it." Marge pauses and looks over at Hayden, who hasn't said anything, but has her nose buried in the bouquet. "Hayden, why don't you put those in some water?"

"I'll help," Graves says, following Hayden into the house.

Bear follows them with his eyes, looking none too happy.

"Guess I screwed up again," I say, partially to redirect an impending murder plot my teammate might be forming against Graves. Obviously, Hayden has been on dates. Overheard Marge and Lisa discussing one of them once. Being deployed so much, maybe Bear has never witnessed it. Not sure a member of our team dating his daughter would be appropriate. Not that Graves is a bad guy or anything.

"What'd you do this time?" Martinez asks, scratching his chest.

"Told Marge and Bear about the kind of diet Riley has to be on so she'd have food she could eat at the party." I kick at the concrete patio. It's hard enough for her to manage what to eat and when to eat it on a daily basis. Social events are harder and might not have any food she could consider eating.

Stephens cocks his head to one side. "Without telling her you were going to do that?"

I nod, still not seeing where the problem is.

Stephens loops an arm over my shoulders and says, "Let's go have a talk."

We walk away from the grill and sit down near the koi pond, away from everyone else. The fish dart in and out, surfacing now and then to grab some unlucky bug on the surface.

"Do you remember that day at Shaken and Stirred? Back

in the early days when Taya and I were first paired up?" he asks, picking up a pebble and tossing it into the pond.

I watch the ripples radiate away in circles. I know exactly what day he's talking about. "Hard to forget that day."

It had been Martinez's birthday and Marge had put together a little gathering. We were getting settled when Stephens's ex-wife's sister Brittney showed up and started talking shit about how Stephens's brains had been turned to scrambled eggs. Before that, none of us had known that he had suffered a traumatic brain injury on our last mission. Well, Bear knew. Nobody else, though.

While it had been at least a little bit entertaining to see Taya and Marge have to be physically restrained from kicking Brittney's worthless ass up one side of Shaken and Stirred and down the other, it hadn't been much fun finding out that my teammate hadn't trusted me with crucial information.

"Yup. Very hard to forget. I was still coming to terms with my diagnosis myself. I wasn't ready to share it with anyone else, but it got shared for me. Without my permission."

"Should have told us yourself. We're a team. How am I supposed to support you if I don't know what's going on with you? What does it matter how we found out?" Until Graves, I had been the newest member of the team and always felt like the odd man out. Well, at least when it came to Bear, Stephens, and Lux. Luckily, I had Martinez. But not knowing about Jim's health when Bear did had been a sore spot for me. Still is.

He turns to face me. "I'd have let you know if and when you needed to know. Point is, it was my diagnosis and my personal information to share. Not anyone else's. Brittney took that away from me just to be cruel."

"But I wasn't doing this to be cruel. I was trying to help."

Stephens shakes his head. "Doesn't really matter. It was Riley's information to tell. Not yours. She's new. Probably doesn't want people to look at her differently. I know I hadn't wanted that. I couldn't stand the idea of being pitied." A shadow passes over his face and I get a sense of how deep his hurt and pain went.

That day still gave me an ache, too, though. "Why would we have looked at you differently? We were all there when that bomb exploded. Any one of us could have gotten unlucky that day."

"I was afraid my brain was never going to be okay. That the damage was permanent. I felt . . . less than." He turns away and tosses another pebble into the pond.

I make a noise in the back of my throat. "Wouldn't have mattered. We're still brothers. You should have trusted us. We can't be a team if we don't trust each other. We don't come back alive if we don't trust each other."

Stephens turns back to me, his brow furrowed. He puts a hand on my shoulder. "I do trust you, but Riley's still learning to trust you. She hasn't even begun to learn to trust the rest of us."

I groan and rest my face in my palms, finally getting what she was so mad about. "And I just gave her a huge freaking reason not to trust me ever again."

"Afraid so. One thing you have to remember, as much as you were trying to care for Riley, you need to communicate with her beforehand. Sharing a person's disability with others without consent—even if you are doing it out of love—is a misstep. It's not your decision to make . . . unless it's a medical emergency, of course."

"What do I do? Do I go after her?" I need to find a way to make this right.

Stephens scratches his head. "Give her a minute to cool down. She probably knows in her head that your heart was in the right place. Let her heart catch up with yours."

Wow. To say that Taya has changed Jim Stephens has got to be the understatement of the century. That was damn close to poetry.

We walk back to where everyone is gathered around the food.

"Well, come on, then," Marge says, clapping her hands. "Let's eat before it all gets cold."

You generally don't have to tell a SEAL team to start eating. Everyone grabs plates and starts to fill them from the dishes set out on the side table. Mason and I end up in line behind Graves, who seems to be frozen over the potato salad. I trace his line of sight and see Hayden standing in the doorway, sunlight filtering through her crazy hair and outlining the shape of her legs through the long peasant skirt she's wearing. I elbow him and he startles, plunking a mound of salad on his plate and moving on to a stack of burgers.

He's a good kid, emphasis on kid. Come to think of it, he's probably only a couple of years older than Hayden is. She's twenty-three now. They're closer to being peers than Graves is to Bear. I somehow doubt Bear will see it that way, though.

I get Mason settled with his plate over by Tony and Inara and go back to the condiment table where Graves is putting the finishing touches on his burger. I knock his elbow and he looks over his shoulder at me. "Yes, sir?"

"I may not be the right one to give advice. Lord knows my own love life is a damn mess. I'd take your eyes off Bear's daughter, though. Touch her and he will kill you." I squirt ketchup on my burger.

Graves's face is about as red as the slice of tomato he spears with his plastic fork. "I, uh, don't know what you're talking about."

I shrug. "Whatever you say, kid." I walk over to the table and take a seat between Mason and Martinez.

"Where's Riley, Dad?" Mason asks, looking around.

"She, uh, had to go." Damn it. How am I supposed to explain to an eight-year-old that his father's an idiot?

"Where?" He looks over at me, mustard smeared on his chin.

I take a napkin and wipe his face. His nose wrinkles under my hands. "I don't know for sure."

Mason's face scrunches up. "Did you guys get in a fight?"

He's a little too observant for his own good, this kid.

"Kind of. I, uh, did something wrong. Didn't mean to, but there it is."

"Are you gonna apologize? Ms. Shapiro always makes me apologize, whether or not I'm wrong." He looks down at his plate.

I've got to get him out of that school. Lisa's barely speaking to me, though. There hasn't been a moment to tell her about what I overheard go down between Riley and Ms. Shapiro at the parent-teacher conference. "I'm gonna apologize."

Martinez claps me on the back. "She'll cool off, man. Give her some time."

I take a large bite of my burger so I don't have to answer.

Buzzing sounds erupt around the table and each member of the team is pulling phones out of pockets.

"No," Marge says. "Just no."

Bear gives her a sad look. "I'm afraid so."

I sigh, looking down at the message on my own phone. The team's been called in. I look down at Mason and my heart drops to my stomach.

Marge speaks before I can say anything. "I'll get Mason to Lisa. She can pick him up when it's convenient or I'll drive him home. Until then, he and Leslie can hang out in the meantime."

There it is. What it means to be a team. I don't even have to ask and someone's there to help. Not just with training or equipment. With my life. All of it. I drop a kiss on Mason's head. We'll be okay.

CHAPTER TWENTY-ONE

Riley

I LEFT THE barbeque, saying only a quick goodbye to Marge, Inara, and Taya. It's a pure wonder I don't get in an accident on the way home. I'm so mad I could spit. Lucas shouldn't have done that. It was a violation of my privacy and it was just plain stupid. He really doesn't get it. He never seems to see when he's about to go too far, push too hard, ask too much.

Sure, he wants to help. He wants to protect. It's who he is and what I admire about him, but that doesn't mean he gets to eclipse who I am and what I want to do. He doesn't always know what's best, especially if he doesn't bother asking.

I pull into the driveway, and when the garage door goes up, I see my board and know exactly what I need to do to feel better. After going inside to change into my bathing suit, then putting on my orange short-sleeve rash guard, I head back downstairs and into the kitchen where I scribble a note on a Post-It, then stick it on the fridge so Lucas will know where I've gone. While I'm pissed at him, there's no need to make him worry about my whereabouts.

I quickly grab my board, and then I'm on my way to the beach.

The drive and briny smell of the ocean, plus the warm rays of sunshine, calm my emotions enough so that when I arrive, I'm able to put all my energy into the task at hand.

"Hey, Riley." Brian waves to me from behind the Gold Star Family Surf School table as I walk up. "I thought you were taking the day off."

"I thought I was, too, but my plans changed. Figured I'd see if you needed any help down here." The one sure thing I've found to get me out of my doldrums and put things in perspective is to do something for someone else. And I can't think of anyone I'd more like to do things for than these kids who have all lost someone.

Brian smiles. "You know we always can use you. Wanna help Allison over there with the twelve-year-olds?"

I look over to where a fit, dark-skinned young woman is showing a group of pre-teens how to wax their boards. "Absolutely." With a grin, I jog over to the group in time to help Allison show them all how to attach their leg ropes.

An hour later, Allison and I start to lead the group into the water. One of the mothers watching the lesson jogs across the hot sand toward me. She waves her hand in the air. "Excuse me."

"Great." The preteen girl with her brown hair braided huffs and crosses her arms after dropping the board to the ground. "Here we go."

My gaze bounces between the girl and the woman.

"I'm so sorry to bother you. But we haven't met. I'm Julie." The woman extends her hand.

I take it and shake. "Riley."

"I just wanted to ask you to keep more of an eye out for Tara. My daughter has Meniere's disease, which causes severe vertigo. Can you please stay close by her side out there?"

"Geez, Mom. Can't you just let me do something for myself for once? Why do you have to tell everyone to watch out for me?"

My brow lifts and I bite the inside of my cheek. How many times I've wanted to scream that at my own mother? How many times I actually did? I glance back over to the woman and nod. "Will do."

Tara rolls her eyes, picks up her board, and makes her way toward the water. I follow, seeing myself as the preteen stomps through the sand and into the surf. Guess I'm not the only one whose loved ones seem to put their business out there.

I stand in the surf, the cold water at waist level, watching all seven of our group bellyboarding toward the beach. One kid even manages to pop up and ride the small wave in. The look on his face is pure delight. I know how that power and connection to the ocean feels and my heart brims with the knowledge I've helped give a kid who's had to face grief at way too young an age an experience he'll be able to enjoy for years to come. For a moment, I try to imagine Mason's face with that kind of smile. I want so much to give that to him, to share my love of the ocean and the sport, but I'm not sure Lucas and I are destined to make it. So much seems to stand in our way. Every time the road in front of us seems clear, another obstacle pops up.

As if my thoughts had conjured him, I turn toward the shoreline to find Lucas standing a few feet from Tara's mother. Great. This was supposed to be my getaway. My place away from any argument. But seems my *husband* decided otherwise.

When I face the kids once more, I spot Tara struggling on the board, her knuckles white as she grips the corners with eyes squeezed shut. After wading over to her, I place my hand on the center of her back. "Are you okay?"

"Fine."

I know that tone. I've given off the same one. Which means the real answer is "no" and that Tara wants the truth to remain hidden. I purse my lips and take a deep, centering breath. Okay, her mother said she had a disease that gives her vertigo. So, severe dizziness.

I take a step back and analyze my surroundings. Tara's board is bobbing a lot in the water, which has become a bit choppy. She's also lying on her belly with her eyes closed. I scratch my head and try to think of a way to help, yet allow her to finish the activity.

"Tara, sit up and open your eyes. I want to try something."

"Don't need your help."

I snort, then catch myself. But my reaction catches her

attention and she glowers at me. I hold up a hand, palm facing her. "I don't find this funny. I suffer from something, too, and you sound just like me. I kinda can relate."

Tara's face softens a bit and she grunts as she lifts her body up. When she sways, I take a step in and place a hand on her back. "See that blond guy about ten feet from your mom? Concentrate on him. Focus on his face."

"He's . . . cute." She blushes a little. "Why am I looking at him?"

"Because looking at your mother would defeat the purpose. It'll just make you angry."

Her shoulders slump forward. We take some deep breaths and just remain out on the water for a few minutes, hoping the spell will pass. Thank God her mom caught me before we headed into the waves. What if she hadn't said anything?

Tara might have been even more embarrassed if everyone panicked, not knowing what was going on. Or she could've gotten hurt by pushing too hard. What if she'd gotten lost in the mix? Sure, there are only seven kids to two instructors, but things happen.

My gaze travels back to my husband. Maybe I'm the reason I was embarrassed today. No one had even mentioned or hinted at anything that made me feel less than. And they had all known before I found out the information was shared.

"What if he'd been deployed and no one had any idea?"

"Huh?"

My eyes widen and I whip my head back toward Tara,

realizing I'd asked myself that question out loud. "Sorry, nothing. So, how are you feeling?"

"Not a whole lot better."

"Well, we are just about done, anyway. Try to paddle on your stomach toward shore. Keep looking at the man and keep a focal point. Usually staring off at one solid thing in the distance helps with balance. I'll stay by your side in case you need anything."

She nods and adjusts herself, and a few minutes later we are back on shore.

Lucas waves to the group, probably goodbye, and starts walking toward me. I turn toward my car. No sense in letting everyone hear our business. Certain things should be done in private. And I'm still angry about the situation, though not as much at him anymore. But I still need some time.

Lucas meets me halfway. "Riley? We need to talk."

I stop and turn. He looks down at the sand, then out at the ocean. Anywhere but at me. This can't be good. "I get you're angry and I'm sorry, but this is about work. I'm leaving for training. There are some things we need to go over."

For a second, the words don't register. Then they hit and I feel my shoulders sag. "Leaving? For how long?"

"Three weeks. Could be longer. Sometimes we bounce from one training to the next. Other times we may be needed somewhere else and are sent out on a mission." He looks up into my eyes now.

I can do three weeks. Even more. No problem. As long as I know when he'll be back. "But you'll let me know?"

"No, not always." He takes my board from me and we continue walking toward the parking area. "I'll call when I can, but to be honest, it might only be once or twice. Can't say any more. Part of the job. Part of this life."

I glance behind me at the Gold Star family kids on the beach. They'd all had a conversation like this. Someone told them they were leaving, but their someone never came back. The reality of what Lucas does hits me like a tidal wave. This is what Marge, Taya, and Inara were talking about. This sucker punch to the gut of not knowing where my husband will be or even if he's okay. "Oh."

"I have to go home and pack." He pauses a moment, then looks at me with a questioning expression on his face. "Wanna help?"

My mouth can't find the words. My lungs can't find air.

All I can do is nod.

CHAPTER TWENTY-TWO

Lucas

WE GET HOME and Riley showers off and changes quickly. I'm downstairs in the kitchen, getting out all the snacks to be packed on the table. Things like sunflower seeds, powdered Gatorade, jerky, dried fruits, and nuts. Also, a few cans of Chef Boyardee.

Riley snorts. "Seriously? Thought you had this stuff for Mason in case you didn't have time to cook."

"You have no idea how useful this stuff can be. Not just to eat, but to trade." I hold up menthols and dipping tobacco. "Same with this shit. I don't smoke. Others do. Will be used to my benefit."

I glance over at her. She's worrying at her lower lip and I want more than anything to stop her with a kiss. But I'm not sure how that will be received. She's talking to me. That's something. It ain't permission for a lip-lock, though. "Taya, Marge, and Inara are here to help. Anything you need. Even if it's just to talk. Take them up on it. Trust me. They're amazing women." This is the part of the job that's tough. The not knowing, the disappearing. Add in that communication can be sparse and eventually most spouses leave. Lisa is a strong woman and she couldn't take it. God, I hope Riley can.

She nods.

Now the part that's a little more muddied. "Might need some help with Mason. Lisa has a lot going on. I added your name to the approved list of people who can pick him up at school if needed."

Riley's expression is priceless, a disbelieving smile and pink in her cheeks. "Lisa was okay with that? Letting me help take care of Mason?"

I nod. "Lisa knows the drill. Has been through it herself. At the end of the day, we are all here to support each other. It's the only way this works." I take a deep, measured breath. "And it has to work, Riley. I'm not quitting my job. Not leaving this life. Please understand that."

Something flashes across Riley's face, but I don't know what it is. She's tough, but this can be a lonely life. It's one thing to talk about the possibility of me being gone for long stretches with no communication, it's another to actually live it. She shakes her head, gathers some of the items in her arms, and heads back upstairs. I follow. When we reach my room, she drops everything on the bed, then spins around to face me, index finger pointed at the mattress. "Dare I ask what all the socks are for?"

"Better to have too many. You don't want to see what feet look like when they're not taken care of. You definitely don't want to feel it either."

She shakes her head and helps me finish packing. Once everything is stowed, we stop and look at each other. I'm not sure what to say. She has an uneasy expression on her face as her hands rub up and down the sides of her jeans. Then she steps toward me, putting one hand on my chest over my heart that has started to beat faster.

I close the distance between us and circle my arms around her waist. "I know you're still angry at me. I wish we had time to resolve the issue before I leave, but we don't. Jim explained to me what your side must be like. I don't think I can ever apologize enough. Just know I didn't mean it in any malicious way."

She nods. Her eyes are wet, lips pressed tight together as if she's trying to keep from crying. "I know you'd never do anything to intentionally hurt me. It just meant so much to me to not have them think of me as sick."

I hang my head. That had been pretty much the screwup to end all screwups. "I'm so sorry."

She rests her head against my chest. "I know."

I tip her chin up toward me and place a gentle kiss on her lips. To my surprise, her hands circle the back of my neck and pull me in closer as her mouth opens beneath mine. My tongue tangles with hers and a bolt of desire shoots through me like lightning. I'm instantly hard.

She leans back to look me in the eye, a sparkle there that makes something flutter in my chest. Her hand slides down my chest to my crotch, cupping me through my jeans. "How soon do you have to be at the base?"

I glance over her shoulder at the clock on my bedside table. I wish I had the time to take her slowly, to worship every inch of her with my hands and my mouth and my tongue, to bring her to the edge again and again and then watch as her orgasm crashes over her. I don't, though. "I have a little time."

She unbuttons the top button of my shirt and says, "I'll take what I can get."

Every muscle in my body tenses as she finishes unbuttoning my shirt and slides it open. Her hands roam my chest, pausing over my nipples, and sending a shudder through me. With her gaze locked with mine, she reaches down and unbuckles my belt. The buttons and zipper of my jeans are undone next and she pulls the hard length of my cock free. Still looking into my eyes, she sinks to her knees. She circles the head of my cock with her tongue and I groan. Her tongue sweeps up and down its length, leaving a trail of warmth behind it. I close my eyes and let the sensations wash over me. Then she takes me in her mouth, its wet-hot heat sending fire through my entire bloodstream. I reach down to cup her head as she slides my cock in and out of her mouth, finding a rhythm like a drumbeat that matches my heart.

After a minute, I can't take it anymore. I lift her to her feet and practically tear her clothes off. In a moment, she stands before me without a stitch of clothing between us and I marvel at the perfection of her. I back her up until her knees hit the bed and she's down on her back. I ditch the rest of my clothes.

I cover her mouth with mine. The sweet tangle of our tongues change into a pillaging. I want more of her. I want to go deeper and farther. She arches beneath me and moans. Still kissing, I let my hand slide to her breast, cupping its weight, my thumb circling the nipple. I'm rewarded with a gasp.

My hand slides lower, over each line of flat, sunken skin. Her scars are living proof of how strong she is, of what a fighter she is. Then I'm between her legs, tracing the line of wetness there. Her legs fall farther open. "Lucas," she whispers into my mouth.

I slide a finger inside her and she bucks against my hand. I discover the rhythm she found with her mouth on my cock, searching for and locating the swollen mound of her G-spot. She undulates beneath me and I kiss my way down so my mouth joins my hand. Still with my finger inside her, I find the sweet mound of her clit with my tongue. She says my name again. Louder.

And then I sweep my tongue into that most sensitive spot, circling and toying as my finger massages inside her. The buck of her hips picks up speed. The blood is pulsing in my ears and in my cock. Then she's pushing me away. I look up. "Did I . . . did I do something wrong?"

Her pupils are so dilated I almost can't see the color of her eyes. "Nothing wrong. You did everything right. Now get up here and let's finish together."

After putting on a condom, I lay on my back and she straddles me, my cock reaching for her like another arm. For a moment, she stays poised over me, the lips of her pussy just brushing against me, driving me wild. I thrust up just as she glides down and I am deep inside her. I grab her hips as she begins to rock on me. Her body undulates above me, her hair a blond river falling over her face as she leans down to kiss me again.

Then she's back up, rising and falling, taking me deeper and deeper inside her warm wetness. I slide my hand between her legs, letting her rub her clit against my knuckle as she rides. Her hands rise to her own breasts, cupping them and teasing her nipples, and I feel myself edging closer to my own climax. "Riley," I groan.

"Yes," she gasps, picking up her own rhythm.

Her pussy squeezes me harder and she rides faster.

"Yes," she says again. Louder this time.

I won't last much longer. I can't. My cock is so swollen for her that I feel like it might split. The feel of her on my cock, the sight of her rising and falling above me, the taste of her still on my lips. It's all more than I can bear. I arch my back, and just as I'm about to explode, I feel the shudders of her orgasm overtake her and she's screaming my name. Her pussy massages me with the last convulsions of her orgasm.

I want to lie there in a tangle of limbs with her forever, but that's not the way this works. I roll to my side and kiss her. "I have to go," I whisper.

"I know," she whispers back.

Silently, we dress, retrieving our cast-off clothing from around the room. Riley giggles when she finds her panties hanging off one of the bedposts and the sound makes me feel like my heart might burst. She's happy. I've made her happy. Once we're done, I carry everything downstairs and drop it at the front door.

I turn and take her in my arms. "I hate leaving you."

"I'll be here when you get back. Don't worry about Mason. Anything he needs, I'll be there for him too."

"Thank you." Her words mean so much to me. I bend down and place a soft kiss on her lips. She deepens it, as if tasting me for the last time. Reluctantly, I pull away. Need to get to base. Being late is not an option.

"See you soon."

She waves and I turn around, pick up my stuff, and head out the door. Done this what feels like a million times. No matter what, it never gets easier. But this is the life I chose, and while there are many amazing parts to it, leaving is one of the parts that sucks.

I shake my head to chase away the sadness. "I'll be home soon enough."

Getting in my car, I turn on the engine and back out onto the road.

Yes, I'll be home soon.

CHAPTER TWENTY-THREE

Riley

LUCAS HAS BEEN gone for two weeks and I've talked to him once. For five freaking minutes. This fucking sucks. Every night as I go to sleep, I hug his pillow to me. There's a lingering hint of sage from his shampoo that invades my dreams with his presence. I miss having those muscular arms around me, making me feel safe and loved. I miss the way he set my body on fire with his touch. My dreams are full of him, strong and tender, but when I wake up every morning, the bed is cold and lonely. I wake up alone. I work alone. I eat alone.

I toss the fork I'm holding down onto the table. No amount of chewing makes these eggs easier to swallow. My mouth is dryer than a sandbox in summer and each passing moment only leads to the next. Not to mention everything I eat tastes like cardboard and not because of the restricted diet.

"Today is just one of those days," I remind myself. Not every day is going to be cheery and I have to remember all the good that has happened over the past two weeks.

Like the fact I started working. It's only part-time and it will be a while before I qualify for benefits, but it's going well and it's a huge step to being able to take care of myself. Also, my volunteering at the surf school has led to picking up some private lessons. I love working with the kids. Passing on my love of surfing to them feels like a gift. I'm thrilled with how I'm making a life for myself here in Virginia Beach, but I know it would be sweeter if I could share it with Lucas. Each step I make toward making my own life here means I'm building the life we can lead together when he comes back.

And the biggest shocker? Lisa called me to help out on a few occasions with Mason. He even slept over one night. I know Lucas would be as happy as I am that his family is supporting each other, but he doesn't know.

Lisa reaching out means she views me as someone she can rely on. That Mason can rely on. And that is the best feeling in the world. For once, no one is viewing me as the weak, sick girl who needs to be taken care of. I'm the strong one who can take care of someone else.

This marriage, being part of this program, isn't a short-term gig anymore. When Lucas comes home, I fully intend to talk to him about my interest in looking past the one-year commitment. I still want to be independent, able to take care of myself, but I want to do that standing at his side.

Speaking of . . . my gaze falls to the reading log I need to sign for Mason. With all the technology that exists and that schools make the kids use, like Google Classroom, I can't believe they still send home a paper form for parents to sign. This could easily be done online. But the school year will be over in two weeks. Maybe the school has a suggestion box. I could make the recommendation for next year.

I can't believe it's already mid-June. What Mason does over the summer? Camp? Vacation? I bite the corner of my bottom lip. Should talk to Lucas about it, come up with a plan in case he has to spend time here. Maybe we could all do something together, take a mini vacation. I've never been to New York.

My phone rings and I reach across the table and grab it, hope making my heart quicken. "Lucas?"

"Sorry, no. Mrs. Craiger, it's Dr. Patel."

Crap. This can't be good. She didn't look so enthused during my appointment yesterday. I'd hoped she was just having a bad day or something. "Hi. I thought maybe it was my husband."

"I understand." She pauses for a moment, then continues. "Mrs. Craiger, some of your test results came back yesterday and I'm a bit concerned. I'd like you to come into the office today. We have an imaging facility on the first floor. I think we need to get a better look at what's going on."

My throat closes up and tears prick at the corner of my eyes. I take a deep breath and try not to get too ahead of myself. "Does it have to be today?"

There's another pause. "Yes. I do feel it's urgent enough you get in right away. I don't want to panic you, but this isn't something that can be put off."

The fingers of my free hand curl into a fist and slam against the table. Yeah, today is one of those really fucking sucky days. And just when I started to think I'd be able to actually have the life I wanted. "What time?"

"Come around noon. You might have to wait. We're squeezing you in."

"Will do." What else can I say? After everything I've been through, no way am I going to prolong whatever imaging or tests the doctor needs to run. The sooner the tests are done, the sooner I have meds that can help, the sooner I feel better.

At least the appointment is early. I'll have plenty of time to pick Mason up from school. Lisa got stuck with some urgent appointment and asked if I'd step in. Hopefully, the appointment's not with her lawyer. Wouldn't that be typical of the day I'm having if I helped Lisa take custody of Mason away from Lucas?

The doctor hangs up and the last of my appetite drops like a stone while my stress levels go through the roof. That was definitely not the call I needed today. Maybe I should forget the idea of traveling to New York.

Three hours later and I'm still sitting in the godforsaken waiting room. Screw the lime-green paint. I know they use it in waiting rooms because it's supposed to remind you of nature and make you happy. It's not cheery, though. It's only irritating. I get that they're squeezing me in, but doesn't anyone realize I have a life? That I have other obligations? That I'm a complete person, not just a case of Crohn's.

I glance once more at the clock on the wall. I need to leave in thirty minutes to reach Mason's school in time. I drum my nails against the wooden armrest. Seriously, how much longer is this going to take?

The nurse comes out from the back holding a folder and I sit forward on my seat and pick up my purse. She calls out someone else's name and I collapse back in my chair as a middle-aged man wearing mom jeans follows her into the back. We play out this same scenario three more times. How many more times will we do it? The waiting room is full. I have no idea how many of these people are going to be called in before me. At this rate, I'm going to walk out of here an old woman.

Fifteen more minutes pass. My heel taps against the floor and my temples pound. I have to make a choice. Either I walk out of here and hope the doctor can squeeze me in another day or I wait. If I leave, what more damage could happen if I need treatment but don't get it as soon as possible? But if I wait, what do I do about Mason? It strikes me how very much alone I am here with Lucas gone. It doesn't just suck to be alone. It hurts. I curl over, holding my stomach.

Lucas's words from when he was leaving come back to me. Reach out. Call Madge or Taya or Inara. Maybe I'm not alone. At least, not totally. I pull out my phone. The phone rings a couple of times before the call connects. "Inara?"

"Hey, Riley." She sounds happy to hear from me and I feel some tension leave my shoulders.

"Don't mean to be a bother, but I'm kind of in a jam." I grimace, hating having to rely on someone else, hating feeling like I'm unreliable, especially when it comes to Mason.

"Sure, what do you need?"

"Lisa asked me to pick up Mason today and I'm stuck at a doctor's appointment. I was supposed to be seen at twelve, but they're running ridiculously behind. Any way you might be able to go get him for me? I can come by your house after I'm finished here to pick him up."

"Absolutely. Just text me the address and what time I need to be there."

I glance up at the clock and cringe more. I'd waited as long as I could. Literally. "Actually, you probably have to leave now. Is that okay?"

"Consider it done." There's some shuffling that comes across the line and then Inara speaks again. "And Riley, don't forget, we're all there for one another and never hesitate to reach out. For anything. We all need a hand now and then."

The meaning of her words sinks in. Asking for help doesn't mean I'm weak. I wouldn't think less of Inara if she asked me for a favor. Maybe admitting that I need a little help doesn't mean I'm helpless. "Thank you. I appreciate this so much."

We hang up and I send her the address. Finally, after taking a deep breath, I sit farther back into my chair and relax a bit. Some of the weight is off my shoulders and I feel the relief of knowing I'm not alone and that the wives of Lucas's teammates are on my team too.

I'm not sure what I would've done if I didn't have them for support.

CHAPTER TWENTY-FOUR

Lucas

I STARE AT my ex-wife's phone number on the caller ID of my phone. Literally have been back in Virginia Beach for five minutes. I haven't even gotten to my truck yet and there she is, making my heart sink down to my boots. It didn't use to be that way. Even after we'd split up. Since she got engaged and moved, though, every phone call has been some sort of argument. I could hit the "ignore call" button. But no, I can't. Mason could need something. I pause in the shade of the hangar where our plane just landed and accept the call, preparing myself for the barrage of how I did something wrong.

"We need to talk."

Yup. Definitely should've hit the ignore button.

I drop my pack to the ground, pinch the bridge of my nose and force my voice to come out as steady and calm as possible. "Hello, Lisa. About what?"

"Your wife."

I grit my teeth. Yeah, fuck no. I thought this was going to be about Mason. If I'd known she wanted to complain about Riley, I definitely wouldn't have answered. "Lisa, you have no say over my personal life. Including who I marry."

"You're right. But I do have a say over who Mason is around. And your wife is untrustworthy. Our son is not in good hands with her." There is a bite to her voice, as if she's prepared to fight.

I take the bait even as I know I shouldn't. I'm exhausted and my defenses are low. This training was hard. Not just due to the nature of the exercise, but also because I hardly got a chance to speak to Riley or Mason. I miss my damn family. I was in a place where I didn't have a second to myself, but I still felt lonely. Now my arms ache to be around them both.

"You have no idea what you're talking about. Riley adores Mason. She'd do anything for him." The damn woman pretty much ripped the head off his teacher, fighting for his well-being. The pressure in my head and shoulders increases. I rub at the back of my neck, trying to release the tension.

"Yeah, well, then explain to me why she couldn't go pick up Mason after she said she would. Riley didn't even bother to call me. Instead, she sent someone else, some stranger. What was so damn important?" Lisa's breath is audible through the phone. "Did she have a date or something?"

That was a low blow and she knew it. Was she really insinuating that Riley was stepping out on me while I was gone? When had Lisa started fighting that dirty? Well, dirty is as dirty does. "Fuck you." I hang up the phone. Damn it.

I've never cursed at my ex-wife. Hell, I've never cursed at any woman before. I was raised in a "yes, ma'am/no, ma'am" household. Well, I did swear at that one nurse that time, but that was because she reset my thumb after I dislocated it. Hurt like a son of a bitch. Mother Teresa herself would have probably told that nurse where she could shove it.

My priority can't be to win a fight, though. It has to be Mason, and for Mason's sake, I need to be on good terms with his mother. I take a deep breath and, opening my text messages, I shoot off an apology to Lisa for my behavior and tell her I will call later. Then I tuck the device into my pocket. This shitstorm is not what I wanted to come home to.

I shoulder my pack and stalk over to my truck, jump in and head home. My foot is heavy on the gas, thanks to the ball of anger swirling around in my chest. Of course, it's only made worse when Lisa's nasty response to my text pops up on the truck's CarPlay.

"We can talk later, but I've already spoken to my lawyer."

"Goddamn it." I slam my hand against the steering wheel. She reported the incident to the lawyer. What the hell did Riley do? I know she wouldn't do anything to endanger Mason. I know it in my bones. Something shifts in my chest. Then again, my bones have been wrong about her before. I gave her my heart and my soul once, only to have her stamp them with "Return to Sender" and walk away. Now I have to go home and grill her about what happened. Again, not what

I wanted to do after the way I left things three weeks ago. The two times we spoke, it felt like we were putting that behind us, that we were back on solid ground. I'd hoped we could stay on that track once I got home, but this is my son, and I won't lose my relationship with him for her or for anyone. She better have a good explanation for whatever she did that's put a bee up Lisa's butt.

I open the truck windows, hoping the ocean breeze will calm me down, but no such luck. Not on a ninety-degree day with the humidity hovering in the low seventies. The air is a damp physical force to fight through and I've had too much fighting already. I rub my hand over my face. That's got to be it. I'm tired. Maybe this isn't as bad as I've made it out to be in my head. Lisa was never one to fly off the handle before, but maybe that's changed.

I'd better follow up and get a few more facts before my mind spins totally out of control. Opening my contact list on the screen, I press my lawyer's number. As the phone rings, I formulate questions to ask, trying to think it all through calmly, rationally. Especially since Lisa sounded anything but. It's a losing battle, though. When the call connects, my stomach plummets, anxiety gripping me by the throat.

"Misoulis, Summers, and Associates. How can I help you?"

"Hi, this is Lucas Craiger. I'm a client of Mr. Summers. Is he available?"

"Please hold and I will check."

The music that comes on the line further grates my nerves. Who thought making a Muzak version of "Don't Worry, Be Happy" was a good idea? The guy in the car ahead of me is driving the . . . Exact. Speed. Limit. Like why? Shaking my head, I move into the left lane and pass the slowpoke. It's not hard, bro. Just press down on the big rectangle.

I shrug my shoulders to release some of the tension. The sooner I get off the road, the better. Driving this anxious, this angry, is not safe. Luckily, I'm not too far from home. Just need to hold on a little bit longer. I take a big deep breath and count to ten as I let it out.

"Mr. Craiger. Nice to hear from you." Dean Summers's voice comes through the truck's speakers.

"Hey, Dean." I take another measured breath. "Listen, just got home from training. Lisa called me pissed to holy hell. Said she reported an incident to her lawyer."

"Yes. I was waiting for your call. Seems your wife, Riley, sent someone to pick up your son when she was supposed to be the one to do it. The person wasn't on the authorized card the school had, so they reached out to Lisa. Took them about thirty minutes to get clearance." There was a pause. "To say Lisa was distressed is a bit of an understatement."

"Who picked Mason up?" Did Riley send Genghis Khan or something? She barely knew anyone in Virginia Beach. Who could she have sent?

The sound of papers shuffling comes through the speakers. "An Inara Martinez."

Okay, this shouldn't be too bad. Tony is actually on the emergency contact card as an authorized person to help with Mason. What's the big deal? "She's the wife of one of my teammates. Her husband is one of the points of contact, in fact. That doesn't seem like something to blow a gasket over."

"Well, Lisa feels otherwise. And it does seem Riley didn't give anyone a clear reason as to why this happened. She'll only say she was held up somewhere and asked Ms. Martinez for help. That's not quite all of it either. Looks like Mrs. Martinez had to actually meet Lisa to drop your son off when he was scheduled to stay with your wife. Again, Riley isn't explaining any of it."

Something about this didn't smell right, but that wasn't really the point. "How is this going to affect the custody case?"

Dean's sigh traveled down the line. "It's not good. Listen, you aren't going to get full custody, we discussed this already. Not with your current occupation. But now they're going to make the case that Mason shouldn't be in Riley's care, that she's not trustworthy with the well-being of a child. That could greatly impede the time and circumstances you are actually around him."

What was Riley up to? Why couldn't she just tell them what was going on? She was making this worse and worse by the second.

God. Fucking. Damnit.

"Listen, Dean. I gotta go. Let me talk to Riley. If I find

something out that may be valuable, I'll update you."

"Sure thing."

We disconnect as I pull into the driveway. I stare daggers at the door, every muscle in my body tense. Sitting here is doing no good. Time to rip this bandage off and see what the hell actually happened. Assuming Riley would explain anything to me. She wasn't always willing to trust me anymore than she trusted Lisa.

My footsteps thud on the steps to the front door. I take a few steps in and drop my pack with an even bigger thud. The air-conditioning provides some relief from the heat and humidity, but not from the tension that's built up in the short time I've been back CONUS. I have come and gone from this house what feels like a hundred times and it's never felt this damn crappy. Don't I get one place in the whole freaking world to relax? Doesn't seem like that much to ask.

I take a few steps farther into the house and spot Riley in the living room, talking to someone through her headset. She looks up from the computer screen and waves. A big smile spreads across her face, only to fall a moment later. She could always read my moods and it seems like she isn't missing how fucking pissed off I am.

"Glad I could help. Have a nice day." She presses a couple of buttons and pulls the headset off. Then she stands and makes her way over to me. "I can't believe you're finally home. Is everything okay? You look upset."

Is she for real? A sarcastic snort escapes my lips. "No, everything is not okay. Care to tell me why that is?"

"I . . . I don't know." Riley furrows her brow, a slight tilt to her head. "I thought I wasn't supposed to know about things that go on at work. Well, the secret stuff, anyway."

Seriously? She thinks this is about work? About the training I've returned from? "This isn't about work. Why'd you send Inara to pick up Mason? Do you know the shitstorm you started?" My voice is loud, booming with anger. Yet, tears prick at the corners of my eyes. I counted on her. I believed in her. Is there a worse betrayal than betraying the trust of someone who puts their child in your care? I don't think so.

"Lucas—"

"I may lose my son, not be able to have any relationship with him at all." My voice breaks. "All because you couldn't show up on time to pick him up for reasons you don't seem to be willing to share with anyone."

"Lucas, I was at the doctor. I needed to get a CT scan done. It was last minute, an emergency. It wasn't like I had a choice. You're the one who told me to lean on the other wives if I needed to and I needed to right then." Riley straightens to her full height.

"Why not just tell Lisa that, then? Why make it a big secret and let her spin lies about it?" Damn it. I get that she wants her privacy, but this is my kid we're talking about.

Tears streak down Riley's cheeks. "This is what I was afraid of when I told you about being sick. Or at least one of the things. I was afraid Lisa would find out and make some kind of case that I couldn't be relied on because of my

Crohn's. Now she's doing exactly that without even knowing the full extent of it. I missed picking up Mason once because of a doctor's appointment that went too long and she's using it against you. Against us."

Dammit to hell. Not what I was expecting her to say. Though, I'm not sure what I thought her answer would be. I pace back and forth across the room, fingers clenching and unclenching, as I try to release the tension and anger from my body.

The situation is all too much. What am I supposed to do?

"I need to get cleaned up." I turn and head upstairs to my room.

CHAPTER TWENTY-FIVE

Riley

I LISTEN TO Lucas stomp up the stairs. A few minutes later, the water turns on. I have a few minutes to think, to figure out what to do here, what's right for me, for Lucas, and, most importantly, for Mason.

So much for the euphoria of life working out. I should have known better. I keep trying to prove I'm more than my disease and my disease keeps shoving me aside to show the world that it's what I am—all I am.

Raking my hands through my hair, I let out an audible groan. Tara was a sign, one I missed. The universe's way of telling me things won't ever be normal. Look what happened to her. Even with me trying to help, the preteen wasn't able to do what the other kids did. She needed someone by her side to help.

Like me. Which means if I can't pull my own weight, I'm nothing more than a burden. Just look at the mess Lucas and poor Mason are in now because of me.

Maybe it's time to stop fighting. Maybe it's time to let him, let them, go. Find someone who is better suited for this family and their needs. Based on what Dr. Patel told me, the next few weeks are likely to be ugly. I'll be even more of a burden, and what if Lucas gets sent away for work again? I won't be reliable. I won't be the strong one. I won't be standing by his side. I'll be curled up in bed in pain and we'd have to saddle one of the other wives to help care for me. Like they don't have their own lives, their own families to care for.

And that's the best-case scenario. If the operation Dr. Patel says I need doesn't go well, if things go sideways like they did with my appendectomy . . . well, it could be months—hell, years—before I'm okay again.

And Lucas will sacrifice everything to take care of me. Though, not sure how much control he truly has when it comes to his job. But I know he'd try, even possibly throwing away all his hard work.

I have to go and I have to make sure Lucas doesn't follow me. I drop my face to my hands. It's a replay of what happened all those years ago between us. I'm going to have to hurt him to save him from himself. To save him from me.

The water's still running upstairs, so I go back to my computer to work. But my mind is a mess. My stomach aches, my heart hurts, and my fingers shake. Why does doing the right thing, the best thing for someone you love, have to hurt so much?

Thirty minutes later, Lucas comes back downstairs. He looks into the living room, but seeing I'm on the phone, he heads into the kitchen. Once I am done speaking with a customer, I disconnect from the call center that transfers customers to my line and head into the kitchen myself to find my husband leafing through the pile of mail on the island and eating a turkey sandwich.

I straighten my spine, hoping the improved posture will give me the strength to get through this. "I think we should talk."

He tosses the phone bill he's holding on the table and takes the last bite of his sandwich. I walk to the island across from him, shoulders back and chin up. "I'm having some problems because of my Crohn's."

His gaze shoots to lock with mine. "Okay. How bad is it?"

His brows furrow, like he thinks this is a problem he can solve. But he can't. I place my hands on the cool granite, as if it can support me both emotionally as well as physically. "It's pretty bad. Worse than I let you think. In fact, it always has been. I've been a mess pretty much since the beginning. My meds stopped working not too long after I moved here."

"That's why your doctor's appointment was an emergency? Why you couldn't pick up Mason?" He looks so tired. I hate dumping this on him right when he's come home from such a long time away, but if I don't do it now, I'm not sure I'll have the strength to do it later. Another night in his arms and I may not be able to make myself leave.

"Yes, and it's why I was hoping I could be part of a clinical trial, get access to some new drugs that might help." I square my shoulders. "It hasn't been easy. The drugs are expensive. So are the scans and the surgeries. It's why I had to rely on my parents for everything. I hated it. I felt like I was suffocating. As soon as I went into remission, I moved to get away from them, but then I had to figure out how I was going to pay for what I needed to stay alive."

He doesn't say anything. He just stands there and listens.

"I started having flare-ups and nothing I was doing helped. Everything that I might be able to try was too expensive. At least, it was with my insurance. But not with the kind of insurance a military spouse gets."

I look down at my hands and fidget. I hate the things I'm going to say next. Time to come clean. Regardless, this was bound to come out sooner or later. "It's why I joined the program." I lift my head and look him directly in the eye, trying to keep the tears from forming in mine. "You kept saying something didn't add up, that I was holding something back. You were right. I joined the program to get health insurance. It's the whole reason I'm here. It's the only reason I'm here. It's why I've been trying to make you believe we're really together again." I watch the impact of my lie hit him.

Without a word, he picks up his keys and walks out the door.

CHAPTER TWENTY-SIX

Lucas

THAT'S IT. STICK a fork in me. I'm done. Thoughts bounce around in my head like bullets ricocheting off steel walls. She said she was here for the duration, that she was in it for real. But bits and pieces of other conversations come back to me. That day in the therapist's office when Dr. Stehman asked why Riley had joined the program and it took her a while to come up with an answer. Her insistence on finding a job as "a backup plan." It wasn't a backup plan. I was the backup plan, the stopgap she needed to have insurance until she got a job with benefits and the benefits kicked in. She wasn't here for the long haul. She didn't want us to be a family. She wanted fucking access to prescriptions she couldn't afford on her own.

She didn't love me. She didn't love Mason. We were tools to get what she wanted, and I'd bet dollars to donuts she was planning to head out the door as soon as she got it. And I'd fallen for it, fallen for the sweet smiles and those sweet, sweet nights she spent in my arms.

She'd promised she wasn't going to hurt Mason, that she

wasn't going to walk out. Yet, here she is, admitting that the only reason she's stayed married to me so far is for insurance. Insurance!

I get in my truck and the tears burst forth like water from a dam, spilling down my face. My chest heaves. I lay my head on the steering wheel, feeling the muscles of my chin tremble against my will. Static buzzes in my head, drowning out my thoughts. I straighten and look out the windshield, as if the sunlight can soothe me. It can't. I'm not sure anything can.

I put the truck in gear and back out of the driveway. I don't know where I'm going, but I know I'm not staying here.

I'm losing my son and I'm losing Riley all over again. The two people in the world who mean the most to me. And there doesn't seem to be a damn thing I can do about it. Every way I turn is the wrong way. Every step I take mires me deeper in the mud.

I have never felt so completely helpless.

I've worked so hard to get where I am, to prove her father was wrong about me and what I could become. I can put food on the table and clothes on their backs and a roof over their heads and it means nothing because this is a problem I can't fix.

I can't fix her medical issues. Can't make her love me. So, in the end, I'm still going to end up alone because all it seems I have to offer anyone is health insurance and a paycheck. And just look at my son—what do I have to offer him? Riley was the one who stepped up. Not me.

I shake my head. One thing's for sure—what little I can offer my son, even if it is just financial security, I'll do it. Because I know what it feels like to be the kid growing up in a family, worrying if we would have enough to eat for the week.

Softly splashing water droplets hit the windshield as my wipers whoosh back and forth. I don't know how long I've been on the road because there was no destination in mind. But it's been long enough that the gas tank starts to get low. Neither the rhythm of the rain nor the trip calms my nerves. And the roads are becoming slicker by the second, which means I need to find another outlet to help calm my emotions.

I tap the button on my steering wheel, which activates the hands-free phone connection. The cabin fills with the loud sound of ringing five times before Martinez picks up.

"What's going on? Everything okay?" He sounds half asleep. Of course he does. Anyone who had gotten back from the training we'd just gone through and who had a lick of sense should be home and in bed after a home-cooked meal and a welcome-home fuck from his hot wife. That's what I hoped I'd be getting for the nanosecond before my phone rang with Lisa's name in the caller ID. Before everything when to shit faster than grease through a goose.

"Nothing good."

"Speak to me." His tone is louder and crisp, as if he's been awake for hours.

"I . . . I . . ." I can't. I can't choke out the words.

A heavy sigh cuts through the speakers. "Pendejo, it's raining and you are driving this upset. Meet me at Shaken & Stirred in twenty minutes before you get yourself killed."

Before I can respond, the call disconnects. Of all the things I am grateful for, my best friend is one of them. We've been through a lot together, survived missions by the skin of our teeth together. So, if there's anyone who might be able to guide me through this minefield, maybe Martinez can.

I beat Martinez to the whiskey bar and restaurant by five minutes. I nod to the hostess as I walk past the wall of polished whiskey barrels at the entrance and through the tables. Neither Taya nor Inara is working. They're home with their husbands, the husbands that they'd been matched with, husbands that they loved for who they were, not for health insurance. I feel a stab of guilt about pulling Martinez away from Inara, but I know she'll understand.

I find a place at the polished mahogany bar and already have two beers sitting in front of me by the time my best friend sits down next to me. He picks up one of them. "Thanks, man. I could use a drink."

"Who said it was for you?" I say, glancing at him from the corner of my eye. Just seeing him makes my heart hurt a little less.

He punches my shoulder. "You sound a little better. You had me worried there on the phone. What's going on?"

I tell him everything. All of it. For once, Anthony Martinez is speechless. Like literally gape-mouthed, staring at me like a calf that has been hit between the eyes with a bolt.

"Just like that?" he finally says. "Admitted it out in the open? She married you for the health insurance?"

I nod and finish off my beer. "Just like that." I signal to the bartender for a refill.

"Dude, I had no idea. Hand to God, I thought the chick was crazy about you and about Mason. Inara thought so too." He shakes his head. "Didn't know I could be so wrong about a person."

I should have known I could be that wrong. I'd thought she was the real deal back when I was in high school. Thought she was as crazy about me as I was about her. Then she'd left me. Turned her back. Sent me away. And I'd fallen for her hook, line, and sinker again. Stupid, stupid, stupid. Wrong, wrong, wrong. What was that old saying? "When someone shows you who they are, you should believe them."

"What are you going to do?" Martinez turns his glass in slow circles on the bar.

"What else is there to do? Go home. Tell her to get out. Pick up the pieces." I put my head down on my pillowed arms on the bar. The thought of sending Riley away stabs at me. Even though I know she's just using me. Even though I know she doesn't love me, I still love her with every inch of my being. Still want to help. And if it was just me, maybe I'd shrug it off and stay married so she could receive health insurance to get better. It's something I could offer, something that would improve her life. And if she stayed for a few months, I'd try to enjoy those few months as much as I could.

But it's not only me in the world anymore. I have to think about Mason. He's already attached to Riley. She's his guardian angel. I can't let him get any more attached when she's going to leave us once she gets into the trial. Or gets better. Or even finds someone else who can take care of her better . . . like a doctor. How do you explain to a little boy that the nice lady who stuck up for him with his teacher doesn't really give two shits about him? That it was all an act?

"Well, if you need a place to stay, we've got a guest room. Inara wouldn't mind. Some days I think she actually prefers your company to mine, being she thinks you are more *mature*. Even though you were also responsible for instigating the pillow fight that lead to the broken vase incident. No way Mason throws that hard."

I snort. Never in a million years would I guess someone thought I was actually more mature than my teammate. Least of all his wife.

Martinez scrubs his face with his hand. The exhaustion is creeping back up on him. It's creeping back up on me too. I need some rest. "Thanks. But I'm good."

I'll sleep in the back of the truck before I do that. The idea of watching Tony and Inara spark and glow at each other while my heart still lays in the wreckage left by Hurricane Riley is too much. I'm happy for my friend, but I don't want my nose rubbed in it right now.

I finish my beer and pay our tab, then head out. Tony

pulls up to the side of my truck with his Durango and lowers his passenger-side window. "Call if we can do anything. Anything. Really."

And I know he means it. He'd lay down his life for me. He's already done it more than once. "I will."

I drive home, rehearsing in my head what I'll say to her, what I want to say to her. My feelings, my heart, and my son's feelings were not something for her to play with. Granted, she wasn't the only one with ulterior motives for agreeing to the match. While I'd signed up hoping to find someone, the benefit of having a person there for Mason to make his life better was the reason I'd agreed to be assigned to Riley specifically in the first place.

So, maybe we both came into this with the wrong agenda. But things changed for me. She was so great with Mason. She really tried to fit in and get involved with not just our family, but the community. Helping those families who'd lost someone in war is important to us all. I admire all those things about her.

It just doesn't make sense why she'd get so involved, especially with my son, if she intended to leave. Why she'd allow him to be collateral damage?

But it ends up not mattering, though. I come home to a dark house and a note on the table. Riley is gone.

CHAPTER TWENTY-SEVEN

Riley

I LET A wave wash over my feet, and it rises until my calves are underwater. The water recedes and sand loosens under my feet as it's swept back to sea. Like the hope I had just days ago. As if my life could work out. My relationship too. But like a sudden squall, the news Dr. Patel delivered violently tore it from my grasp.

"The scar tissue has formed a stricture. Surgery is highly recommended, especially to prevent intestinal blockage."

Every muscle in my body freezes except my heart, which is hammering so brutally against my chest it might crack a rib. My lungs refuse to expand, and my nails dig into my five-foot shortboard.

I figured surfing would clear my head, help me make sense of things, help me get out of my mind a bit. It's also the reason I grabbed as much of my stuff as I could the other night and went to a hotel. Thought the time away, the solitude of my own room without Lucas, might bring my options into focus. But it didn't, so here I am.

I close my eyes and listen to the waves crashing on the

shore, beckoning me. I imagine them beneath me, lifting me, pushing me forward like wind behind a sail. Calm begins to wash over me.

When my muscles relax, I open my eyes and look out. The ocean ripples with shades of blue and fringes of white foam. A salty breeze brushes my cheeks and pushes my hair off my shoulders.

I dive in with my surfboard, paddling hard before pulling under the breaking waves. There's a heaviness in my belly that has nothing to do with water pressure. Each time I resurface, I force this morning's conversation deeper into the back part of my mind.

As another set of waves approach, I study them, looking for the peak. I lie on my board and paddle to position myself where the wave will be fullest.

The first one is weak, so I wait for the next. As the second wave approaches, it grows more powerful and I turn the tip of my board toward shore. When the water starts to swell, I paddle hard, then spring to my feet in one swift movement.

In that moment I am a bird, gliding over the sapphire sea, free from life's problems. I feel alive. I reach out and drag my fingers through the water as if trying to touch heaven itself. I launch over the crest, then plunge into the water.

After resurfacing, I climb back on my board and straddle it, sitting up. I dip my hand into the ocean, letting the crisp water run through my fingers and secretly hoping it had the answers to all my problems. I feel the pulse of the sea beneath me, a repetitious and soothing rhythm.

Being out here always makes me feel strong. Powerful. I am fragile against the force the sea can dig up and hit me with. But every time I get knocked off my board, I climb back on and stand back up.

I breathe in deep and hold my breath before exhaling. My throat tightens. Lucas has no idea what I went through during the last surgery. The pain. The mess. The despair. While Dr. Patel said this one wouldn't be so bad, there's no guarantee. Hell. I went in for a simple appendectomy and it turned into a medical emergency that has upended my life for years.

None of this, however, is Lucas's problem. He has plenty of his own already. The big one—Mason—should be where his focus is. I thought I could help him. I thought I could be there for Lucas and for Mason, yet all I've done is make it all worse. I could be the reason Lucas loses custody of his son. Me and my stupid Crohn's disease.

Surfing, unfortunately, isn't life. The surge and power I feel while I'm on my board are fleeting, ephemeral. The truth is that I'm not powerful and strong. I'm Riley the Sick Girl. I'm the girl with Crohn's.

Which is why I know what I have to do, what the right thing is. I came into the program under false pretenses. I needed the medical insurance. Then life delivered Lucas back into my life and I fell in love with him all over again.

Actually, I don't think I ever fell out of love with him. I'd just pushed those feelings down as far as I could and left them behind.

He should have stayed in the past. It was best for him then, and it's best for him now. Especially with Mason. I won't make him give up his job, not when it's his calling. Nor will I add more stress to his life. Lucas and Mason need someone who can be there for them at full strength. Someone who can do after-school pickup and overnights and show up at soccer games. Someone who can be reliable and pull their own weight.

Someone who isn't me.

I head back into shore. I sit down on my towel and grab my phone. Time to do the right thing. Once the screen is unlocked, I punch in the number to Lieutenant Graham, my point of contact for the Issued Partner Program.

The phone rings. And rings. I'm about to hang up when he finally answers.

"Lieutenant Graham speaking."

"Um, hello, Lieutenant. This is Riley Thompson. I mean, Riley Craiger." My voice is shaky, the pitch a little higher than normal. Not that I'm second-guessing my decision. Just nervous about the fallout.

"What can I do for you, Mrs. Craiger?"

Mrs. The twist of the knife. "I want to drop out of the program, end the marriage."

Nothing but silence.

After a few seconds, he responds. "Are you in danger? Were you harmed?"

"No. Nothing like that."

"Then may I ask why you're looking to leave the program?"

My fingers tighten around the phone. No sense in beating around the bush. I suck in a deep breath and try to center myself. This is for the best of everyone, not just me. "Lieutenant Graham, the marriage is not working. There's too much history there, too much with the family Lucas already has. The stress is affecting my health and impeding my ability to control my illness. I'm sorry, but I do think it's in everybody's best interest for the marriage to end."

He grunts.

I clear my throat. "I'm sure you got the therapy notes from our session. There is a custody hearing going on as well. Lucas's ex-wife hasn't taken to me. I don't want to bring more harm to a young child if I can help it. I volunteer with a program that helps Gold Star families. I've seen how much kids in military families deal with."

He sighs. "I understand. We do need you to come by and sign the paperwork."

"Of course." I listen as he goes into detail about how my benefits will cease immediately, along with some other legal stuff, almost as if he's trying to find any source of hope I might reconsider. Not that he knows Lucas or me or what our love means to me. He just wants to make sure the program succeeds.

I disconnect the call and toss the phone aside, allowing the tears welling up in my eyes to finally fall. My shoulders shake and I rest my head against my knees, curling into a tight ball.

This will hurt Lucas. I hate that. But if I stay, I'll be hurting Mason, too, and hurting that little boy means hurting Lucas even more. There's not much I can do about it. Lisa hates my guts and has from the second she laid eyes on me. Nothing is going to change that, and as long as I'm in the picture, she's going to push to keep Mason away from Lucas. I've seen the way that little boy looks at his father and the way Lucas looks at him. I would never ever intentionally do anything to take that away from either of them, not even for the true love that I think I've found. Not when it means risking a little boy's happiness.

I force myself up onto shaky legs. Once I've packed everything up, I grab my board and head back to my car. After brushing off the sand sticking to my calves, I swap my sandals for sneakers and jump into the driver's seat.

Time to leave what I've built here behind. There's one more call I have to make. The one I'd fought so hard not to need to do, but one thing I've learned is that sometimes we all need a little help, someone to guide us through choppy waters. Someone grounded to focus on as we maneuver toward shore.

When the click of the call connecting cuts through the speakers, I suck in a sharp breath and say, "Hi, Mom. I'm coming home."

CHAPTER TWENTY-EIGHT

Riley

THROUGH MY BEDROOM window comes the brightness of the sun. I soak in the warmth and my spirits lift as I do. I roll to my side, dangle my legs off the side of the bed above the off-white carpet on the floor. I use my arms to push myself into a seated position. My surgery was successful, but I need to be careful with my abdominal muscles for a few more weeks. I rub my knuckles in my eyes, stretch my arms above my head, and yawn. Grabbing on to the post of my bed closest to me, I hoist myself up. It gets easier every day. I take a moment to be grateful for how well everything has gone.

After wrapping a robe around myself, I head downstairs into the kitchen where my parents are sitting and having breakfast, crossing my fingers today won't be the day they decide to finally chastise me for marrying Lucas. Sure, I waited until the day before surgery to tell them exactly what had gone on in my life. And while they had a moment of venting their disapproval, their focus was on my upcoming procedure. They still haven't really brought up the subject again, to me, but who knows what has been said behind closed doors. Today may finally be the day. Crossing my fingers it isn't, though, because my emotions are still too raw.

The morning light filters through, making the threads of silver in my mother's blond hair glint. How long have they been there? And those lines around her eyes. Have they always been there? Dad's changed too. It's not just the gray in his hair. His forehead is more creased than I remember it. He's still a big man. Nearly as big as Lucas and certainly as bullheaded, but his shoulders slope in a bit more than I remember. He looks up from the newspaper he's reading and immediately slaps it down on the table. "Why are you out of bed, Riley? You should have used the intercom. It's why we had it in installed, for Pete's sake. Mom would've taken food up to you."

Here we go again. From the moment I stepped off the airplane, they've done nothing but hover. And try to control as much of the situation as possible. While Tara's mom hovered that day on the beach and informed me of what her daughter's limitations were, she didn't jump in the water and try to take control of the situation. If only my parents would give me some breathing room.

I lock eyes with my father. "Dad, I can walk. Doctor DeSilva told me to make sure I move around. Walking downstairs on my own is going to help my recovery, not hurt it. Are you really trying to interfere with the doctor's orders?"

He grumbles, then looks pointedly at my mother, who

stands immediately. "Riley, darling. Go sit down and let me make you something to eat. If you want, we can go for a walk outside later."

I wave her off, then open the fridge and begin to pull out the ingredients I need to make pancakes. "Please, I really don't want to fight about this. It's just a little breakfast. It's not like I'm out in the barn lifting a heavy bale of hay."

"Why do you have to be so stubborn?" My mother comes up behind me and takes the eggs and milk out of my hands. "Let me help before you hurt yourself."

I grit my teeth and force air out through my nose. My hand shoves the refrigerator door a little too hard and it slams closed. My father's chair scrapes against the tile and I whip my head sideways. He's glaring at me, arms crossed and brows furrowed.

I throw both hands into the air. "What?"

"Watch the attitude, Riley." My father's tone is low, a warning. I'm pushing him too hard.

Well, that's just too damn bad because he's pushed me even further. I jut my chin out. "Why? You going to kick me out?"

Good Lord, I sound like a teenager. I feel like a teenager. Tears gather in the corners of my eyes. I'm a grown woman and they won't even let me make myself a stack of stupid fucking pancakes. All the reasons I left here in the first place are playing out right here and now.

He stands from his chair and takes a step closer. "Don't be ridiculous. You are my daughter, and you will always have a place here, but you will not be disrespectful to your mother."

"Then how about you respect that I'm an adult who can take care of herself? I'm not Michelle." We almost never speak of Michelle, yet her presence is everywhere. Her death cast a pall over us that has never lifted. My parents had become overprotective after she died, and then when I got sick, that overprotectiveness went into hyperdrive.

The sound of glass shattering fills the air and both my father and I turn. What once was an embellished butter dish lies in pieces across the floor. My mother stands over it, hands over her face, shaking. I scurry over, careful to avoid the mess. Should have put slippers on. Damn it. "Mom, I'm sorry." I take her arm and move her backward, away from the jagged pieces of glass as my father grabs the broom.

I slip my arm around my mother, but she pushes me away. "We almost lost you." Her voice is hoarse and ragged with pain.

"But you didn't, Mom. I'm right here." I stand in front of her, willing her to really see me.

"Yes. You're here. You showed up at our door as weak as a kitten on a rainy night. Hurting in both body and spirit." Dad doesn't turn to face me as he sweeps.

I take a step closer. "I'm not weak, Dad. I was sick. It's different. I'm not fragile. I needed help for a few weeks, and I asked for it. Kind of like the way you needed Mom and me when you broke your leg after that colt threw you. Does the fact that we had to help you then mean you're never allowed to do anything for yourself? That we shouldn't allow you to dress yourself and bathe yourself because there were a few weeks when you couldn't do it? Are you weak because you needed help?"

My father jerks back as if smacked. He'd hated every single time he needed to ask one of us for help. His pride had taken a beating each time he'd leaned on us to get up the stairs or accepted the food we brought him on a tray. He hadn't been able to wait to do everything for himself again.

Just like I want to do what I can for myself now.

Yet, my own words start to resonate. Guess my father isn't the only bullheaded one in the family. A trait that is both a blessing and a curse, giving me the strength to fight for myself, but got in the way of asking for help when I needed it.

"That was different, Riley," Mom says.

I turn, brow quirked up, and pin her with a stare. "Was it? Was it also different when you had your gallbladder removed and Grandma came to help? Are you never allowed to leave the house without an escort in case you might need another surgery? Are you now permanently damaged and in need of constant care because you were ill once?"

She steps back, blinking rapidly, but remains quiet.

I tap my toes and cross my arms over my tender middle. "The answer is no. Neither one of you is weak. You're the strongest people I know. Guess what? I'm not weak either. So don't treat me that way. I needed help and I asked for it. That's a sign of strength. Not weakness. And it could happen again. I could need another surgery, or a new treatment, or a place to rest while I recover from a flare-up. I'm going to have Crohn's for the rest of my life. I want to know I can lean on you when I need to without giving up everything."

"Of course you can lean on us. It's what we want. It's why you're staying here, where you belong." Dad straightens from sweeping the broken glass into the dustpan. "You may not like to think of yourself as fragile, Riley, but you are. We don't know why all this started in the first place or what might set it off again."

I want to weep. "We do know, Dad. Doctor DeSilva said that the abscess probably formed because of my appendix perforating and that led to septicemia and now to here. To Crohn's." I bend over a bit too fast to get the griddle from the cabinet beneath the stove and the soreness in my stomach makes me grimace. I hide my face so my parents don't see it, because if they did, it would be another point of contention, another thing they'd use against me.

"And why did you end up with a perforated appendix, Riley?" Mom takes the griddle from my hands and bangs it down on the stove. "Because you refused to tell anyone you were in pain and let us take you to the hospital. Maybe if we'd gotten you there earlier, if we'd known you were suffering, we would have gotten you treatment and none of this would have happened. But you didn't say a word. What choice do we have but to watch you like a hawk? I can't lose another daughter, Riley. I simply can't."

My heart breaks a little at the crack in her voice as she

speaks, but it doesn't change anything. "And I can't live my life in a bubble, Mom. Why do you think I moved to Virginia?" I shake my head. Are they even listening, even trying to understand? Do they even see me?

Dad crosses his arms over his chest. "Well, at least you had the sense to come home where you belong and where you need to stay."

I sink down into a chair. "I'm not staying, Dad."

His eyes bulge. He turns and with great precision dumps the broken glass into the waste can. Somehow he's scarier when he's quiet like this. I almost want him to yell at me again. "And who precisely do you think you're going back to, Riley? To Lucas? Who will take care of you when he's off God knows where for God knows how long? For Pete's sake, Riley, he hasn't even called you since you've been home. Do you think he even cares?"

The tears that threatened earlier are hot as they make their way down my cheeks. Yup, today was indeed the day for my marriage to be discussed—or fought over. And to make matters worse, Lucas hasn't contacted me in the two and a half weeks since I've returned home. But I haven't tried to contact him either. Hell, I didn't even say goodbye. Hightailed it out of there while he was out so he couldn't stop me, because if he really understood what was going on, he would have tried. And if he tried, he might have succeeded. Lord knows, I wish I could have figured out how to stay.

Talk about being between a rock and a hard place. Lisa thought I was unreliable because I hadn't shown up to pick up Mason. If she found out why, she could use my illness as proof I could never be relied on. Damned if I did and damned if I didn't. Staying in Lucas's life meant putting more barriers up between him and Mason, and I couldn't do that to either of them.

"You're wrong, Daddy. Dead wrong. Listen to me because I want to be crystal clear, I didn't leave Lucas because he couldn't take care of me. I chose to leave. I was protecting him and his son. I felt it would be better for him and for Mason at the custody hearing if I was gone. So while I appreciate the help while I'm recovering, I ask—no, I demand—you abide by the boundaries I set, including not speaking negatively about my former husband."

My heart stutters at those last words. I'd received the paperwork to formalize my decision to leave the program before my surgery. My parents had been nosy but I told them it was in regard to ending my lease. Luckily, they didn't push because that would have given them more time to argue with me. I'd mailed the paperwork out right away as I didn't want to impede any custody decisions with Lucas that might have been occurring.

The starch leaves my father's shoulders. My mother turns off the stove and goes to stand next to him. The united front they've presented my whole life. No matter what.

But I'm not done speaking my truth. "And it's not just about him. I've been volunteering to help kids who'd lost a parent to war. Gold Star families. Out on the water, they smile, open up. They share things. They trust me." Tears start to well in my eyes at those last words. Mason trusted me too. Enough to open up about what he was struggling with. "I may not be like most others, but I do have purpose, a life of my own."

Dad's posture falters and he lets out an audible sigh. "We never thought you were weak, Riley. Not after everything you've been through, the way you've fought tooth and nail every step of the way. We're just trying to protect our baby girl like you were trying to protect Lucas's little boy."

And without knowing it, or expecting it, my father gut-punched me. Because suddenly, I do understand. I understand why they would do anything to protect me because I would do anything to protect Lucas and Mason. And Lucas would do anything to protect me, except I took that opportunity away from him. I made the decision for him like my parents had done to me on many occasions.

I hug both my parents, earning a startled *oof* from both of them. "I love you," I whisper. Then I go upstairs, get out paper and pen, and start to write a letter.

CHAPTER TWENTY-NINE

Lucas

I RUN THE side of my thumb along a line of the fake woodgrain on the conference table where I sit across from Lisa. Jayla, the mediator, clears her throat and I snap back into the room.

"And both of you find this agreement acceptable?"

When Jayla first came in, I thought she was too nice. Her facial expression and tone were caring, almost like that of a kindergarten teacher. Figured she wasn't going to understand what my life was like or how being a SEAL worked, and she wouldn't see anything from my point of view. I was wrong. As soft as she appears, and as understated and calm as her voice is, Jayla rules the room with an iron first. Lisa and I both learned not to step out of line while she presided over the mediation. No name calling. No accusations. No assumptions.

All Jayla's interested in is what's best for Mason. In the end, it turns out that was all Lisa and I were interested in too. It just took us a while to see that from the other one's perspective.

I nod and Lisa says, "Yes. It's acceptable."

Jayla smiles, revealing a small gap between her front teeth. She stands up. "I'll get the paperwork for you to sign together. You should be hearing from me in a couple of days with the finalized agreement." She pauses. "I want to thank you both for staying focused on your son throughout what can be a difficult and contentious process. Not everyone can do that, but you two did. It shows what a good team you can be as parents, even if you don't want to be married to each other anymore."

I look over at Lisa. Pink stains her cheeks. I mumble a thank you and the mediator leaves the conference room.

Lisa and I stand too. I hold the door open for her. As we walk out, she says, "Well, that was easier than I expected."

"Sure was." I'd anticipated a lot more push back from Lisa about how much time I wanted to spend with Mason and how I wanted to arrange it. She'd come in loaded for bear, but had gotten a lot less combative with Jayla continually bringing us back to what really mattered: Mason.

Lisa stops at the door that leads out to the parking lot. The glass has a slight mist on it from the humidity outside, but I can still see the magnolia tree dropping fat, pink leaves onto my truck. "I never wanted to keep you and Mason apart, you know."

That was news to me. "Sure seemed that way at the time." I step back and jam my hands into my jeans pockets, waiting for her to go on.

"I know you love Mason and he adores you. I don't want

to stand in the way of that."

I fix her with a look and then gesture back at the mediation room behind us. "Then why did we have to go through all this?" I don't say it with rancor in my voice or in my heart. I honestly want to know.

Lisa blows out a breath. "It was Riley. And the shock of the situation, of finding out you were married without you even telling me, that there was this woman I didn't know personally who was suddenly going to be in our son's life. A woman who you told me about, and not in a good way."

Looking back, I should've handled the situation differently all around. Lisa might've still been guarded against the program at first, but I had Tony and Jim to explain the inner workings if needed. My lack of communication ended up causing a nearly catastrophic issue Though, not sure she would have felt at ease with the Riley match. And I can't blame her. I did open up to my first ex-wife about my high school relationship during our marriage.

My chest tightens. *First* ex-wife. The paperwork ending our participation in the program was filed and according to what Redding relayed during our meeting it would take four to six weeks for the annulment to become official. Then again an annulment means the marriage never existed, so Riley wouldn't legally be considered my ex-wife. Doesn't change how it feels in my heart though.

I blow out an audible breath. "Should have let you know when I signed up. But you could've let me talk to you about Riley. Or we could have come up with a temporary solution if that was a point of contention."

She traces a finger down the condensation on the inside of the door, drawing a snaking line in the mist and laughs, but it doesn't sound like she really thinks anything is funny. "I want you to be happy, Lucas. I really do. Just a shame you ended up with Riley, who left at the first sign of trouble with no explanation, just like all those years ago. And now Mason is affected by her actions."

I can understand her perspective, but I want Lisa to know she's wrong about Riley. That I was wrong about Riley. The letter that arrived yesterday morning from her made it clear. "If it wasn't for her, Mason might still be getting tormented by the kids at that school. They might still be telling him every day his dad didn't love him and had walked away from him. He'd be growing up thinking his father didn't care about him. Is that what you want for him? You know what a father's love means to a boy."

Lisa drops her hand from the door. "What are you saying?"

Now it's my moment to be surprised. "You didn't know? The teacher didn't tell you about what happened at the parent-teacher conference Riley went to? Mason didn't say anything?"

"Not a word from either of them." Her eyes narrowed. "Or from you."

I look down at my feet. "We weren't exactly talking calmly to each other at the time." In fact, every time we spoke back then, we fought.

She groans. "You're right. I own some of that. Now tell me what happened at the parent-teacher conference."

I fill her in on the way Mason had confided in Riley, but not in either of us, and how Riley had stood up for him with a teacher who had been hell-bent on blaming him for the cruelty of other children.

Lisa shuts her eyes for a moment and when she opens them, I see a glisten of tears on their surface. "I didn't know. Poor Mason. No wonder he was getting in so many fights."

"Riley is the one who cleared all that up."

"What about when she was supposed to pick him up and didn't show? And sent Inara instead without a word to me." Lisa lifts her chin. She's not ready to concede. "I can't rely on someone who blows our kid off whenever it's inconvenient for her to show up."

"She was ill. Had an emergency doctor's appointment. And she didn't blow off Mason. She made sure someone he knew and trusted and who loved him would pick him up. I'd say that made her more reliable than most during a medical emergency. She made sure our son was taken care of."

"She didn't tell me she was ill." Lisa shifts her purse to her other shoulder.

"She was afraid you'd use it against her, against me. That you'd say she was too sick to help care for a child."

Lisa shakes her head. "I feel awful, Lucas. I didn't know any of this. I thought she was playing with your feelings and Mason was part of her manipulation. I didn't realize how much she was there for him."

I sigh. "Well, now you do."

Not that it makes any difference. Riley's gone. I lost her.

Again.

"Where is she, Lucas?" Lisa asks, bringing me back to the moment.

I shove my hands into the pockets on my suit pants. "She dropped out of the program and went home to Texas. She needed another surgery and decided annulling our marriage and going home was best so she didn't cause any more trouble for me or for Mason."

And I let her go.

"Why didn't you tell me any of this before?"

"Some of it I just learned today. She, uh, sent a letter explaining her decision." So typical of Riley. A handwritten letter.

My ex-wife closes her eyes for a moment and rubs her left temple. "Let me get this straight. She left you and the program because she cared so much about you and Mason that she didn't want to get in the way of your relationship."

I nod.

Lisa pauses, the muscles in her face softening. "Do you love her?"

I nod again, not trusting my voice to hold.

Lisa steps in and smacks me on the shoulder. Hard. "You idiot. Go get her."

My eyes go wide. "What?"

"I said, go get her. You've been in love with that girl your whole damn life, from what I can tell, and now you're telling me she loves you back? And that she's willing to put her own happiness aside for the sake of our son? What on God's green earth is wrong with you? Go get her." Lisa pushes the door open and marches out into the parking lot, leaving me with my mouth open.

I follow more slowly, making my way to my truck. "What do I have to offer? Really? Just look at us, at this current mess."

Lisa spins around, eyes narrowed. "First, don't pin this on me solely. Remember, you divulged a lot about her over the years. About how she broke your heart, about how her family judged you and yours. I'm part of your family. We have a son together. Your parents were my in-laws and I adore them. What was I supposed to think, to feel? Not to mention you certainly need to work on your communication skills."

No sense in arguing. Part of all this is on me. Well, most of it.

"And second,"—Lisa throws her hands up in the air dramatically—"you are so focused on the hurt from your past, from the circumstances of the way you grew up, you aren't stepping back to see what you have to offer. That is for you to discover. I can ramble off a list, but it won't make a difference if you don't figure it out for yourself."

Once again, Lisa has a fair point. It's not like she hasn't told me things over the years, only for me to question them. To question myself.

I shove my hands into my pockets and clear my throat.

"Need a favor?"

She quirks a brow but remains silent. I rock back and forth on my heels. "Can you not mention anything to my parents? Haven't exactly told them anything yet."

Lisa crosses her arms in front of her chest. "I gathered, especially after they made a comment about how they'd hoped you'd find someone again."

"What? When did they say that?"

Lisa's arms drop to her sides. "When I told them that I was engaged. It was about time they knew, especially when they offered to come up during your last deployment and I turned down the offer. Didn't want them to feel it was personal."

"Oh." I scratch the back of my head. "How'd they take it?"

"They were a bit melancholy, especially your mom." Lisa steps closer and places a hand on my shoulder. "But I reinforced we are still family."

I nod. "Thank you."

"Now, go get your girl…and tell your parents before it slips out."

We say our goodbyes, and I get into my truck and crank up the A/C. After taking a moment for myself to clear my head, I pull out the letter from Riley that came in that morning's mail and read it all again.

Dear Lucas,

I didn't have the courage to finish what I needed to tell

you before I left. I know you might tear this up without reading it, but I'm hoping you don't. I'm hoping you'll read it to the end.

I did join the program for the health insurance. I saw it as a way to get what I needed until I could manage to get it for myself. I couldn't take another second in my parents' house with my mother and father hovering over me, watching every second for something to go wrong. I ran from them and then had to face the consequences of doing that. I was desperate. I heard about the program and leapt at it like it was a lifeline.

And it was a lifeline. A literal one. Because of my condition, I can't be without healthcare for long.

Then Lieutenant Graham told me I was assigned to you. I tried to get him to match me with someone else. I'd hurt you before and I didn't want to hurt you again. I didn't want to hurt me again, either. Breaking up with you and sending you away was one of the most painful things I've ever experienced and you've seen what my stomach looks like. You know what kind of pain I've endured.

They were vehement, though. This was the match they'd made, and they'd made it for a reason. If I wasn't going to follow their suggestions, maybe I should get out of the program. I couldn't risk that. Like I said, I was desperate.

Then I saw you and spent time with you. I saw you with Mason and I saw your tenderness. I saw you with your teammates and I saw your capacity for joy.

I'm not going to lie about this. I saw you and my body responded in ways that I had forgotten it could. You made me feel like a woman again, Lucas. A whole one. You made me feel strong and sexy and confident for the first time in years. Then I got the call from Dr. Patel and I knew that strong, sexy, confident Riley was a dream, and I was getting my rude awakening. I'm not strong and I can't lean on you for everything I need.

I love you, Lucas. I love you more than I can say. That's why I had to leave. I had to have another surgery. There was no way around it. Not if I wanted to live. It's turned out to be just one surgery, but at the time there wasn't a guarantee, and I knew how very wrong things can go. After all, I went in for an appendectomy, something they do hundreds of times a day with no problems, and I've been in and out of hospitals ever since. I know not to count on the law of averages to give me a good outcome.

And there's one more thing. With all the surgeries and no guarantee I won't need others, somewhere along the line I decided I didn't want to have children. But I shouldn't make it seem like it's only because of my health. Truthfully, I've never had the desire to have my own children. I don't hate them. Hell, I love and adore Mason and was super happy to be a stepmom to him.

You deserve a woman you can rely on, not one who has to rely on you. Someone who will be open to expand-

ing your family. Mason deserves a stepmom who can be there for him one hundred percent all the time. I want to be that person, but I can't, and Lisa is going to make sure you and Mason pay for that. I can't have that. I love you both too much.

I'm not going to lie this time. I see now how much pain I caused you by not explaining why I broke up with you before. I thought I was making it easier for you to walk away, but instead, I made you doubt yourself and the kind of man you were and are. You're a good man, Lucas. That's why I asked to be released from the program. I hope you find the kind of woman you deserve, whether it's through the program or not.

All my love,
Riley

I refold the letter and realize I've done nothing but go around in a big circle. Pushed myself physically and mentally to be part of one of the most elite forces in the United States military, only to find that, emotionally, I haven't traveled an inch.

Fourteen years ago, Riley ended our relationship because she was ill and didn't want to put that responsibility on me. I'd walked away without a backward glance. Maybe if I had fought for her, I would have known what was happening and could have proved to her—and to her father—I was man enough to take care of her. I hadn't, though. Hadn't even tried.

Turns out I wasn't the kind of person I'd want my own son to be with. I'd want someone to fight for him. To at least try.

Now Riley's doing the same thing again. Cutting herself off from me so I can go forward unencumbered. Well, Goddamn it, I don't want to be unencumbered. I want Riley. I want her in my life, in my house, in my arms, and in my bed.

And maybe there might be limitations of what I can offer because of my job. Limitations in what I can offer Riley, in what I can offer Mason. But what I can do for both of them now is to lead by example. To show my son not only how to love, but how to show that love.

Which means there's only one thing to do.

I'm going to go get my girl.

CHAPTER THIRTY

Riley

I SINK FARTHER into the mattress and pillow, my eyes focused on the envelope lying on the nightstand. Its contents didn't hold words of sympathy or love or understanding. Just legal jargon that the annulment was official. Yet, the letter cut deep. If only those words included information on how Lucas's custody issues were going maybe I'd feel better. Maybe I'd feel justified in my actions.

But I don't know and therefore, no relief exists from the nagging feeling I made the wrong decision.

"Get the hell out of my house!" My father's baritone voice reverberates all the way into my bedroom upstairs and pulls me from my melancholy stupor.

"What the heck?" I get out of bed and head toward the staircase curious as to who the hell he is yelling at. Though, also because I need a distraction from rereading the letter for the twentieth time in less than twenty-four hours. My father growls loudly and I swear the grand chandelier shakes. Daddy is clearly fixing to open a full can of whoop-ass on whoever is the target of his wrath. But who could have him so worked up? Maybe one of the horse trainers?

I freeze on the landing, gripping the banister, when a familiar voice catches my attention. A low growl whose rumble I feel in my very bones. "There isn't another man who will love her as much as I do."

Lucas.

My heart beats faster. I suck in a breath and head down the steps toward the ground floor.

"Love doesn't pay the bills, young man. It doesn't make sure she gets to the best doctors and has access to the most up-to-date treatments and medications. It doesn't sit by her hospital bed after a surgery or nurse her until she's back on her feet," Mom says.

They're all down there together.

I take a second before turning the corner that leads from the foyer into the living room. When I finally do, air rushes from my lungs. He's here. He's actually here. Lucas. He's come back for me. His broad shoulders make the living room look considerably smaller. I inch closer, partly because I'm in shock, and partly because he and my father are still squaring off with one another. Part of me wants to step in and settle this between them, but they need to work out their issues. The two of them need to come to terms with each other without me playing referee.

But the floorboard squeaks and the three of them spot me. Lucas slips his hands into his pockets, his gaze shifting from me to the floor and back again, as if he's struggling to keep it focused.

"Lucas." When I say his name, his gaze rests on me and heat rushes through my body. His handsome face, always so serious, stays turned to me even as his shoulders hunch a bit. For a second, I see Mason too. I see the bit of boy inside the man and my heart nearly bursts.

"Riley, go back upstairs. Your mother and I will handle this," Dad says, turning away from me, probably assuming I'll do as I'm told.

Lucas goes rigid, but remains silent. We were in this exact same circumstance years ago. I made the mistake of sending Lucas away, then. Not this time.

"No." I step closer until I'm standing at Lucas's side. "I told you when it comes to Lucas, this has to stop. It was my decision to leave, and that does *not* make him a bad guy."

"You didn't have to leave, Riley. You should have given me a chance." While the timbre of Lucas's voice is warm, his words are shaky.

I face him and meet his gaze. "I didn't want to be a burden. I needed another surgery and there was always a chance I'd need another surgery after that. Lisa lost it when I had Inara pick Mason up one time. What was she going to do when she found out I might be in and out of the hospital for a while? That I might never be able to always be there. That there are limitations to what I can do. It's bad enough putting you in a position where you might have to take care of me. To have my illness also mean that you might lose all custody of Mason was more than I could bear."

"Your father and I still don't know why you signed up

for such a program." My mother makes a *tsk-ing* noise, then narrows her eyes and turns to Lucas. Her voice grows sharp and mean. "Did you put it in her head? Was there some benefit you got out of this?"

My hand flies up, palm in my mother's line of sight. "Mom! Enough!"

Lucas takes that hand in his, then lowers it, and takes a deep breath. "No. I didn't put anything in your daughter's head. Riley told me she joined the program because she needed health benefits." He holds his hand up when my mother opens her mouth to speak. "Said you both were suffocating her instead of letting her live the life she wants. She didn't want to take anything more from you, and joining the program was a way to get the insurance she needed without relying on you."

My father growls while my mother rolls her eyes. "Ridiculous."

It wasn't though. Even being back home, it's difficult for them to truly understand. How do you get someone to see that you want their love and support, but still need some autonomy? I can yell, talk to them rationally, or even write a letter about it. But at the end of the day, until they can come to accept it, to recognize it on their own, it's like fighting a never-ending battle.

Lucas squeezes my hand. "There was no guarantee she'd end up with me. She didn't even know I was in Virginia. But it happened. And I fell in love with her all over again."

He reaches out and turns my chin with his fingers to

make sure our gazes are locked. I tremble at the way those words shake me at my very core. But Lucas isn't finished.

"You are the only woman I've ever truly loved. You're a great stepmom to my son. You should have told me what was going on. You didn't even give us a chance to work it out. To come up with a plan together."

"But Lisa—" I start, only to have Lucas cut me off.

"Lisa understands. She didn't have all the facts before. Made a judgement based on prior knowledge, one I can understand that I contributed toward. At the end of the day, she only wants the best for Mason. Just like you and me." He pulls me a step closer to him and warmth rolls off his body.

I look down at my feet, still not quite ready to meet the heat of his gaze. "I can't always be there for Mason. Crohn's is unpredictable. I don't always know what's going to set off a flare-up or when a doctor's appointment is going to run long."

"Then I'll be there, or if I can't, Marge, Taya, and Inara will." Lucas steps closer. "And guess what? My job limits me. You had to attend that parent-teacher conference because I couldn't. Hell, I even missed Mason being born. Does that mean I love him any less? Or that he needs me any less?"

My father clears his throat and I pin him with a glare. This time he actually heeds my warning and remains silent. I bite my lower lip and exhale hard through my nose. "They all have their own lives. I don't want to be a hindrance to anyone."

Lucas laughs. "Hindrance? Who do you think was in the

delivery room with Taya when Otto was born? Because it wasn't Jim. We were away for work. Being there for each other is what the wives do. They're their own team. And they adore you." He pulls me in and wraps those muscular arms that I love so much around me. "Listen, leaning on someone when you need help doesn't make you weak, Riley. Trust me, SEALs know that better than anyone. I've carried teammates out of the field, and they've carried me. I don't think you'd ever call any of us weak. We call on each other's strengths when we have to and step up for each other when we're needed. You can turn to them for whatever help you need. You can come home for help like you did this time if you want, too. Just because you want to be independent, doesn't mean you should exclude your parents."

My father coughs as if he choked on something. Yeah, I'm sure he didn't expect that. My mother's face is red and she's twisting her hands together. "Maybe we misjudged, Carl," she says, glancing at my father.

Lucas shifts and his muscles tense. There's more. He lowers his gaze away from mine. "But none of this matters if you don't feel what I have to offer is enough for what you want for your life. I have my limitations, based on my job and my son, both of which are important to me."

Is this man for real?

I reach out and place my fingertips under his chin, lifting his face so his eyes meet mine. "Lucas, you are way over the top enough and I am so lucky. We both don't have a *normal* life. But what you try to give is more than many who can, actually do. And during this time, I've also learned how much like my father I may be. A big ole stubborn streak seems to run in my family's blood when we get our mind set on something."

He chuckles and steps away from me and toward my father. "Sir, I know you feel I'm not good enough for your daughter, but I love her with everything I have. My son loves her. We aren't a complete family without Riley." He stands straighter, reaching his full height. He is a towering column of a man, strong and proud. He's a living, breathing warrior and he's here to fight for me. "Mr. Thompson, while Riley can make her own decisions, I would still like to ask your permission to ask for her hand in marriage."

What. The. Hell.

Did not see that coming. Figured he might ask me to move back, take things slow. Date even. But not this. My mouth opens and closes, but no words come out. Tears stream down my face, but not from sadness. Maybe shock. Do people cry from being shocked? My father looks past Lucas to me. I can't read his expression and I'm not sure what is running through his mind, but he keeps staring at me. So, I nod.

He growls deep in his throat, but then gives Lucas a curt nod.

It's too much. My father backed down. He conceded to Lucas. Then my mother steps between them and wraps her arms around Lucas in a hug. My whole body shakes. I'm overrun with emotion. Love and relief and hope and joy leave me light-headed, and the man hasn't even asked me to marry him yet.

As if he can hear my thoughts, Lucas steps forward and gets down on one knee. "Riley Marie Thompson, will you do me the honor of being my wife?"

I'm crying so hard no words will form and when I attempt to take a step, I collapse onto my knees. Lucas gathers me in his arms and places a soft kiss on my head. He holds me for what feels like minutes. Maybe it was that long, because all of a sudden, my mother is offering me a box of tissues.

Lucas leans closer and speaks in a soft tone. "As for the other part of your letter. With everything I've gone through myself, I'm perfectly okay with Mason being my only child. Not sure I'd want to be a dad again knowing what I know now and how my job is."

I pull back to look him in the eyes. "What if you change your mind?"

Lucas quirks a brow. "What if you change yours?"

He's got a point. It has crossed my mind about what would happen if something happened to Taya and Jim. Neither have family outside of the group they can depend on. Though, Bear and Marge would be the most likely to be the legal guardians of their son. But what if Tony and Inara have kids? Lucas is Tony's best friend. And I would totally support welcoming their kid into our family if it came down to it. So, maybe my mind might change one day, especially with all the ways there are to expand a family.

I wipe my face and pull away from Lucas. His brows furrow, but I pat his hard chest. "I'll be right back."

While I want to race up the stairs to my room, my pace is slow, thanks to the incisions that are still healing. Each step takes extra strength and I begin to realize that my parents might not be completely ridiculous. Maybe taking it easy would be in my best interest. But later. Right now I need to do this. I have to do this.

Once inside my room, I pull a shoebox from my closet. Then I grab my wallet from my purse and pull out the love letter Lucas wrote to me all those years ago. I take a few breaths and mentally prepare myself for both Lucas and the trek back downstairs.

When I make it to the landing, everyone is standing at the bottom of the staircase. Lucas bounds up to me and scoops me into his arms. "Uh, why are you pushing the limits here? Your mom said you shouldn't be walking around so much."

I scrunch my nose and purse my lips, shaking a finger at him, but he laughs and carries me downstairs. Once he sets me down on my feet, I open the box. "I kept every letter you ever wrote me. This one I've kept in my wallet. I've read it every day I was in a hospital and every time I couldn't remember what hope and love felt like. This letter gave me strength."

I unfold it and read:

I liked you the second I saw you and my feelings are growing stronger and stronger every day. Every new thing I learn about you makes my love grow. Sometimes I don't think I can love you more, but then you do something brave and smart and kind and I do.

My mother makes a strangled noise and I realize that she is sobbing. My father's eyes are wet and so are Lucas's. My own aren't exactly dry. At least we're all crying together.

Lucas takes my hand and kisses it. "So? What's your answer, Riley? Will you marry me? For real this time. Because we choose each other and not because someone else chose for us?"

While I was hoping to draw out the suspense a bit more, I can't stop the huge smile that spreads across my face. "Yes."

Lucas kisses me. Hard. With tongue. In front of my parents.

They better get used to it because there is no way in hell I want my husband kissing me any less passionately because of them. Ever.

Now, if only I could heal faster because there is a lot more than kissing I want to be doing with my once again future husband.

Who knew a military spouse-matching program would give me a second chance with the man I have loved my whole life?

EPILOGUE

Lucas

Two Months Later

I LEAN BACK on my elbows and let the sun warm my face. Seagulls call to each other overhead and a breeze blows in off the water, cooling my skin. I pull myself back up to a sitting position and look out to the water. Riley and Mason bob in the waves on their boards. I can't believe how fast she's healed. Granted, Mason has had to intervene on occasions when she'd become a bit stubborn with asking for help. But I've learned it's harder to say no to a little boy trying to help his stepmom. Probably because assisting seems to have helped my son feel needed himself, feel like he has a purpose.

And as a parent, there's no greater power than helping your child build their confidence.

My parents even offered to come up and help. But Riley didn't want a big fuss made over her. And while I love my parents, they're still angry at me for not filling them in when Riley and I got married. If they did visit there'd be a whole group of people they could join who were upset over the fact

I kept my involvement in the program a secret. And one thing is certain, Tony would only stroke those flames to watch me squirm.

Mom is ultimately happy. She even came to do some basic yoga routines with Riley when we were still in Texas. And when I left because of work, she continued to visit Riley at her parents' a couple of times. Supposedly, my mother-in-law has signed up for my mom's class at the local studio. Never saw that coming, but glad they are getting along.

If only our fathers would follow suit. But Mr. Thompson isn't the only one with a stubborn streak. My father is just as bad. Not that he is against my relationship with Riley. He just wants nothing to do with her father and refuses to step foot in the same room as the other man. Not too worried, though, because there is no way my mother will allow him to miss my wedding. Or start a fight with the bride's father.

I smile and watch as my fiancé and son spring to their feet. The wave isn't huge—even I could probably stay up on it—but Mason's posture changes as he glides toward the beach. He stands a little taller. My guess is he feels a little bit of the power that Riley talks about when she tells me what she loves about surfing.

He's also been standing taller a lot now that he's back at his old school. I really appreciate the sacrifice Lisa's making. It adds to her commute, but in the end, she agreed with Riley and me. Mason needs to be at a school where the staff and the kids understand the special challenges faced by military families and the even more pressing ones faced by kids whose fathers are SEALs.

Riley's been standing taller, too, since she started the new medication. It's only a trial, but so far it seems to be helping her. She says she's having less pain and her appetite has even increased a bit.

The two of them saunter up and plant their boards next to where we've set out our towels. "How was it?" I ask.

"Awesome," Mason says, plopping down next to me, water still dripping from his hair. "It was like I was flying."

I smile and toss him a towel. "Hungry?"

"Starving!" He shakes his head like a puppy getting dry, spraying water everywhere. Riley and I both laugh, something we always seem to be doing, especially when she attempts to play video games. Never seen her suck at something so badly.

"You're always starving these days," she says to Mason. "Somebody's growing."

Mason puffs himself up a little more. "I'm the second tallest boy in my class!"

Riley looks at me from beneath her eyelashes. "I'm not surprised. Look at who your father is, after all."

Mason looks over at me, too, water beaded in his eyelashes. "Yeah. I guess Dad is pretty tall."

Riley opens the cooler and pulls out the lunches she made for all of us this morning. Turkey-and-cheese sandwich for me. PB&J for Mason. A hard-boiled egg and some carrots for her. It doesn't look like enough to me, but she says it's better to eat a bunch of little meals than two or three big ones. She knows what she has to do to stay well. I trust her to do it and to let me know when she needs my help.

Mason tucks in, barely chewing before he takes another bite. "Easy there, champ," she says.

Then she pulls an envelope out and hands it to me. I smile at her, running my fingers over the smooth paper.

"Go on, then," she says. "Read it."

I open the envelope and unfold the letter.

Dear Lucas,

I feel like I'm living a dream and I never want to wake up. For years it felt like I was trapped in a nightmare. Nothing felt real except the pain and sadness of what had become of my life. I was too weak to fight the way life pushed me one way and then the other. I doubted if I'd ever be able to stand on my own two feet. As soon as I was well enough to leave home, I did, but I was sure the only way to be strong was to never lean on anyone.

Then the Issued Partner Program put us together. I was sure it was a terrible mistake. Now I know better. Those folks know what they're doing!

Back when I sent you away all those years ago, I thought it was the strong thing to do. I thought I was protecting you from having to take care of someone weak. Now I realize how cowardly it truly was. Real strength comes from being honest, from showing the people you care about who you really are and trusting that they will still love you. You've taught me that. You've showed me that real strength comes when we lean on each other.

I feel whole for the first time since I went in for that first surgery. I'm not just one thing. I'm not just Riley the Sick Girl. That no longer defines me. My love for you and for Mason is what defines me now, and I couldn't be happier.

Always and forever,
Riley

I fold the letter back into thirds, careful to match each crease up, and slip it back in its envelope. Then I pull the envelope I have for her out from under my towel.

She smiles and holds it to her heart for a moment before opening it and reading it. I know every word I wrote.

Dear Riley,

I've spent years trying to find the right path for these big old feet to follow. I've been all over the world, but nothing ever felt quite right. Somehow I always managed to feel that what I was doing was wrong, not good enough. No place felt like home.

Not anymore. Falling asleep with you in my arms, waking to your smile, walking next to you on the beach always feels right. Every step, every breath, every beat of my heart tells me that I'm finally in the right place. Home is wherever we are together.

All my love,
Lucas

She folds her letter away carefully, too, then rises up on her knees to give me a sweet, soft kiss on the lips.

"Ew!" Mason says. "You two are so lovey-dovey all the time. It's gross."

I tousle his hair. "Get used to it, Munchkin. This is how it's going to be forever."

"Forever?" He ducks away from my hand. "And seriously? Letters? On paper? Who does that anymore? You can just text. Or email."

Both Riley and I laugh.

"You, sweet boy," she says. "Have a lot to learn."

If you enjoyed *Assigned*, you'll love the other books in….

THE NAVY SEALS OF LITTLE CREEK SERIES

Book 1: *Issued*

Book 2: *Matched*

Book 3: *Assigned*

Available now at your favorite online retailer!

MORE BOOKS BY PARIS WYNTERS

Love on the Winter Steppes

ABOUT THE AUTHOR

Paris Wynters is a multi-racial author who writes steamy and sweet East Coast love stories that celebrate our diverse world. She is the author of *Hearts Unleashed*, The Navy SEALs of Little Creek series, *Love on the Winter Steppes*, and *Called into Action*, and is represented by Tricia Skinner at Fuse Literary.

When she's not dreaming up stories, she can be found assisting with disasters and helping to find missing people as a Search and Rescue K-9 handler. Paris resides on Long Island in New York along with her family. For fun, Paris enjoys video games, hockey, and diving into new experiences like flying planes and taking trapeze lessons. Paris is also a graduate of Loyola University Chicago.

Thank you for reading

ASSIGNED

If you enjoyed this book, you can find more from all our great authors at TulePublishing.com, or from your favorite online retailer.

CPSIA information can be obtained
at www.ICGtesting.com
Printed in the USA
FSHW010104160621
82293FS

9 781954 894242